CHILD of

FEAR & FIRE

G.R. THOMAS

First Published 2021
ISBN: 978-0-9945069-4-8

Editor: Full Proof Editing
Cover & Interior: Platform House
www.platformhousepublishing.com

Books by G.R. Thomas

The A'vean Chronicles
(In reading order)

Awaken
Surrender
Allegiance
Redemption

Child of Fear and Fire

This is a work of dark fantasy created to entertain the reader and whilst not intended to cause distress, it may do so for some readers. This story contains fantasy violence, supernatural themes, death, talk of self-harm and non-graphic sexual abuse. If anything in this story causes concern or distress, please contact a support service in your community.

To my husband and children, who sat around the dining table one night under candlelight after the power went out. You helped me work through my story idea, and under the gentle flicker of that candlelight, Child of Fear and Fire found its feet. Thank you and I love you.

Galdrewold
Fictitious English Forest

(Galdr): Old Norse word for spell or incantation.
(Wold): Derived from the old English word, Weald,
meaning forest.

CHILD of FEAR and FIRE
By G.R. Thomas

Fear rouses wicked things. It uncoils an ancient hunger, casts a rancid breath upon the wind in search of the vulnerable. Wicked's tide ebbs and flows at the shoreline of the weak. It oozes into cracks, tends to pains of the soul, draws fear into its dark ocean. It mothers and protects, moulds and nurtures fear, until it becomes something altogether unimaginable.

ONE

It's strange what the mind does when death claws for you. Eliza didn't see flashes of life's joys, achievements or highlights. Instead, fear mastered her thoughts, resentment burned into her soul. She wondered only if death would be less painful than life.

Eliza held onto the only things anchoring her will to stay in this world. The burn of twine bit into her palms and a bitter cold ached up through her toes from the frigid water below.

Darkness yawned its hungry maw for her flesh. Eliza scrambled to stay above the water, clawed at the rope that sliced without mercy. Eliza's wordless sobs echoed around her. Tears dripped from her chin and slid down her throat. The rope shook; her body swayed like a pendulum. She kicked out; her sodden boot slid against the slimy wall of the well. Water sloshed out of the bucket she clung so desperately to — *drip, drip, drip.*

Fear was a deep pain that trembled through Eliza's body. It leached from her skin and stuck to her clothes. It tasted salty on her trembling lips, stung her eyes and clouded her vision. Fear intensified; it twisted her gut as she imagined how deep the water was below and what it would taste like when she drowned.

Terror eked from her. Desperation coalesced in the snowy puffs of each exhausted breath. Fear melded to her screams; it mirrored her, clung to her, then cleaved a part of itself away. Its miasma circled its way up the stone walls, swirled past three vindictive smiles peering over the edge of the well. Fear tasted them on its way past, fed on their rage. It coiled around them, thrived upon their nastiness, then spiralled upwards towards the sky, slipped along the morning breeze towards the hedgerow and deep into the sleeping Galdrewold.

Panic tightened Eliza's calloused fingers. They cramped at the knuckles and weakened by the moment, desperately wrapped around the rope that held both her and the bucket aloft. She could feel the hunger of the well water, imagine it pushing itself into her lungs. *Would it hurt?* The thought drew the veil of unconsciousness over her, but even that reprieve was denied as a drawling voice echoed down.

"I'll raise the bucket if you promise to tell fat old Mrs Embrey that it was you that took the tartlets yesterday," Margaret, the older of the sisters, pulled back on the rope again. The aged whiskers of it brushed her cheek; its ancient plait held Eliza's life in its grasp. The bucket plunged a few feet. Her foot slipped and grazed the top of the cold water again. Her toes curled in her boot. She screamed louder as she swung precariously, the stone walls suffocating, the water a dark eye watching, waiting for her. Eliza's arms shook as she tried to pull herself back into the pendulous bucket. The rope slid again; wetness wicked up the hem of her dress. It weighed her down, pulled her towards the darkness. The depths of the well watched on, glistening with patience beneath her.

Fear consumed her, paralysed her will, immobilised her thoughts, engulfed her voice. Breath carried only her guttural moans for mercy. The sisters had tricked her again, promising her something pretty, a relief from torment if she went down the well to retrieve something that was never there in the first place.

They let the bucket plunge and pulled it to a hard stop at the last moment. Laughter mingled with the splash of water. The freezing shock winded Eliza. Her hungry gasps for air echoed back. *Did death sound so loud?* The water sloshed hungrily at her body until a breath finally filled her lungs again. She bobbed waist-deep, clinging with the last of her strength to the rope before the bucket heaved upwards in awkward tugs. Eliza's body banged against the slimy walls. Bruises swelled quickly on her delicate skin. Her cries were a thousand voices that echoed over and over, trapped, unable to escape, a prisoner, just as she was.

The bucket lurched a little faster. Eliza nearly lost her balance, only saved by the one leg she had wrapped around the rope. Her whole body wobbled backwards; her head smacked against the rocks. Pain ricocheted through her head, but it couldn't mask the acidic voice of Margaret.

"Well?" Margaret shouted down into the depths. "Will you confess?" She dropped the rope again. The bucket splintered under Eliza's foot. She felt it begin to give way underneath her. Warmth spread down her legs; a metallic taste filled her mouth.

The bucket lurched up out of the water again.

"Cook will surely give you a good whipping, but that's to be expected of a servant," Margaret called down, all too calmly. Eliza's hands slipped, her palms shredding by the moment. Her sleeve caps lapped up her blood. Her sobs deepened, her consciousness again slipping away. Eliza's whole body began to numb, her fingers began to uncurl. She let one leg dangle over the side of the bucket. Her eyes rolled. Everything was a blur. Sound slowed and dulled. Her head felt like it was under a pillow. Exhaustion nipped away the rage that wanted to rise within her. Fear, however, remained her master.

Laughter circled its way down the well shaft and slapped away the haze of her concussion. Her fingers curled tighter around the flaxen twine, and she spat the taste of blood from her mouth. She blinked away the sleep that wanted to claim her and squinted at the glare of the light above.

"Tell that fat old witch that it was you who stole from the kitchen, or I'll tell Mother you took them." Margaret leaned deeper over the ledge. "Think you won't be dropped on the steps of a Brothel? Might find your mother there!" The sisters laughed hysterically. Their blurred faces were an evil smear against the small sphere of blue sky.

Fear tempted Eliza again to the comfort of unconsciousness, to a place where the pain was eclipsed, where everything was safe and numb. She closed her eyes just for a moment, imagining the reprieve, but then blinked hard awake when her foot dipped back into the icy water. If she drowned or was dismissed, they would turn on their infant brother, the next in line without a voice. Eliza's belly churned with a stronger flicker of anger. A small fire she never stoked, but it was there, nevertheless. It burned a little brighter for fear of what they could do to such a tiny innocent —

And that which feasted on fear rejoiced in her anger.

"She's too dumb, Margie." Annabelle laughed with delight and dropped her arm over the well's edge, pointing down at Eliza with her doll. "We should just drop her like this." Annabelle released the doll that hung from a noose of ribbon. The doll breezed limply past Eliza; the splash below shuddered through her. Shivering in her soaked clothes, Eliza rationalised a whipping was better than drowning, it was better than the cold fingers of fear that slithered through her veins, and it was certainly better than being cast out to the street where it would be a Whore House for a living.

A slapping sound drew Eliza's eyes away from the doll that floated below. Sybilla, the middle sister, punched one fist into another, much like a street urchin itching for a fight. She had taken to slapping Eliza around the very day Mrs Embrey had brought her home to Norlane Hall, six years prior when she was a scrawny ten-year-old. Eliza remembered the confusion, the shock of a beautifully dressed young girl beating her. That was the first day that fear slipped around her heart.

Sybilla was as clever as she was vicious, always careful to hit her where the bruises wouldn't show. Fear grew day by day since the very first punch to the gut, and she often flinched out of reflex when Sybilla simply walked by.

"Are you listening down there?" The crack of Sybilla's knuckles sounded like bones breaking. "We could just say you're a witch in church come this Sunday. Burn or hang? Perhaps a stoning to death? Do they still do that?" She shrugged her puffy-sleeved shoulders, looking to her sisters as though it was a perfectly reasonable query.

The rope creaked; its bristly twine unravelled a little above her strained fingers. Eliza gasped for energy to pull her weight above the weak spot. Her exhausted groans were cut through by Sybilla's emotionless voice. "Tell the old bat you stole the tartlets. I'll not miss Lady Henley's garden party because of a pastry." All three nodded before the rope was let slip again. Eliza's feet were back in the water. The porcelain doll bobbed against her boot. It rolled over as the water rippled; its cracked, eyeless face glared back at Eliza. It looked as haunted as she felt.

"*Did* you steal from the cook?" Margaret yelled. Eliza imagined Margaret's tongue forked, like a snake's, that was the sound of her voice.

Another thread of mildewed twine snapped and curled over the back of Eliza's hand. Eliza began nodding her head in agreeance to the lie that would save the sisters from social exclusion. Her eyes were glued to the horrific doll face. It spun slowly on the surface; its delicate dress weighed it down until it began to loll to one side. It bobbed unexpectedly. Something seemed to tug at the doll. The water rippled as though something dwelled in the depths. Eliza squealed again when a flash of white snatched at the doll. Bubbles rose and popped around her. It disappeared.

Eliza's muscles cramped in horror. She could swear with each pop of a bubble; she could hear a sound, a whisper, a word. She squeezed her eyes and shook her head. *I'm going insane,* she thought.

She looked away, up to the surface, so impossibly far away, and pulled wildly on the rope.

She yanked her leg away from the touch of something. The doll popped back to the surface; Eliza screeched again. A small star was scratched into its face. The water rippled once more before the bubbling ceased and the doll slowly sank away again... gone.

Fatigue shook her arms, but she found the strength to tug one last time on the rope, crying for reprieve.

"You will confess?" Sybilla asked calmly. Eliza nodded until her neck ached.

The rope creaked and frayed some more. The bucket swayed and banged new bruises into her as it jolted up the length of the well. Eliza held on for her life until she was tipped out onto the ground, coughing and crying, spitting the lichen taste of the well out, gasping for fresh air.

Her raw fingers clawed gratefully into freshly cut grass. The cool eased the sting. She dug until she felt soil slide under her nails and breathed in the sweet tang of the grass. She wouldn't look up as the sisters laughed.

"What is that smell?" Margaret giggled.

"Must be some dirty, stray dog nearby," Sybilla responded. "Ooh, smelly dog, smelly dog," Annabelle sung and danced around Eliza, who was still bent over on the grass. She knew all too keenly that she had soiled herself with fear. The acrid smell of her own bodily waste was impossible to ignore. Humiliation overrode fear for just a moment. Her cheeks burned; her skin felt too tight; the only release was to peel it away, to rid herself of the pathetic shell that she was. She gulped back the urge to scream at them, to pull their hair, to spit in their faces, but she was flat out on the ground, the toes of their shoes too close to her head.

The perfect hems of their dresses swished around her face as they jumped up and down, laughing harder. The cool ground tempered the buzzing under Eliza's cheeks. A thudding ache dug into her ears and clawed its way around the back of her head. She just wanted to get away, to run and hide.

Eliza wiped her eyes with the back of her hand and coughed. She sniffed back her emotions and pushed herself onto her hands and knees. She glanced sideways at them, only briefly, biting her bottom lip until it stung. The sisters held their bellies, overcome with the joy of her debasement. The three young women were well beyond the age of childish cruelty, but yet, instead of preparing their manners for marriage, they seemed more intent on the art of torture — and Eliza was their daily prey.

A mid-morning sun beat down on Eliza's head, easing the headache a little. A gentle wind swept through her mousy hair; her cap lost in the well. She sat back on her legs and wound errant, soaked curls behind her ears. She shook out her soiled apron and slowly stood; every muscle ached. Her bloodied palms smoothed her black dress down to her ankles, her chin quivered uncontrollably, a monstrous beast that betrayed her. A large tear slid from her lashes and settled in the corner of her mouth. She licked it away and sniffed the others back whilst re-lacing her sodden boots.

"Oh there, there," Margaret said, tilting Eliza's chin up, the glare of the sun stunning her vision for a moment. Blues and greens smudged her peripheries until Margaret's pale complexion came into focus. Eliza stiffened. Margaret twirled a dark ringlet through her fingers, an expression of mock concern plastered across her face. Eliza focused over Margaret's shoulder towards the immense hedgerow and wished she could hide behind it, away from them, away from everything.

"Worry not; we are all friends." Margaret's mutterings brought Eliza's attention back from the grand divide between the perfect gardens and the wild forest beyond.

"You know we merely jest with you, Eliza?" Margaret's brows curved innocently upwards whilst Sybilla crossed her arms, fists snuggled in her elbows. Annabelle smiled sweetly, twisting a ribbon around her own wrist until her fingers bloomed scarlet.

Eliza nodded quickly and curtsied to the sisters. Their unspoken threats were as palpable as if they'd beaten, drowned and hung her with the inference of their words.

"Good girl." Margaret patted Eliza's head as if she were a dog, then wiped her hand down her side as though she'd touched something unspeakable. "Let's just keep this all to ourselves, Eliza, and tomorrow we will make it up to you dear, you know, for saving us the humiliation of missing the garden party."

Eliza's eyes flooded. She stared at a single little clover missed by the gardener's scythe. Their kindness always came with a sting. Her heart pounded against her ribs, new tears fell to her boots, soaked with her own waste and water. Her foot slid to the right and squashed the clover from existence.

"Come with us on our adventure tomorrow. I may even lend you one of my bonnets, that is, if you wash that stink off yourself!" Margaret screwed up her face and pinched her nose.

Eliza's head swam. What was this new cruelty they had planned? An adventure with them was never a joy for her. Her fingers clutched the edge of her apron and plucked at the frayed threads. She peered at Margaret through the curtain of her loose hair. Margaret's cupid lips pursed into a tight, vindictive smile. "What say you, dear Eliza?"

Eliza couldn't so much as blink, let alone answer. Every day she wondered if it might be her last. Which day would be the day they'd kill her by accident or design?

Sybilla tapped her knuckles together. "Do you want more of the same? Play with us or let us play with you?"

Eliza nodded quickly, picked up her heavy dress and ran for the kitchen, almost looking forward to Mrs Embrey's switch.

TWO

Eliza tossed and turned that night, waking numerous times to prod the lumps in her mattress, but comfort evaded her, and sleep wouldn't stick. She lay there many an hour, exhausted, staring at walls. In the light of day, they were a worn grey, a tone that suited the room and her life. Bland and colourless was how she felt. The bloom of youthful exuberance had withered within her. No light lay ahead; darkness mastered the past, and the present was an unfulfilling nothingness sandwiched between an uncertain future and torturous upbringing. Eliza was a grey figure in a black and white world of rich and poor, cruel and kind. Somewhere in between everyone else, she merely existed, plain and ignored.

Between the vagueness of sleep and consciousness, Eliza sat bolt upright, heart thrashing for an already forgotten nightmare. She reached for her water, gulped it quickly and patted around the bed, looking for her sleeping cap. She plucked it up from the floor and tucked it under her pillow, too tired to put it back on. She flopped onto her side, pulled the covers up, yawned and stared towards her door, always sure to keep her back facing the wall.

A glimmer of hallway light flickered beneath the locked door as though someone was passing by. She pulled her covers tighter and watched for the turn of the doorknob. Her fingers found the rough patch on her wrist. She picked until she felt the slipperiness of blood. The sting was a relief, the scarring a reminder that she had control over just one thing. She sniffed the air, no hint of brandy, her nails released her skin. The shadow disappeared, the rigidity in her limbs relaxed.

Moonlight cleaved the floor of her small room almost all the way to the door. Her eyes dared to leave the entrance and followed the lustrous glimmer back towards the window. The moon's silvery disc shimmered between the lace curtains. She rubbed her eyes and pressed down on her bloody wrist with the sleeve of her shift until the bleeding stopped. One of the older wounds had scabbed darker than usual. Her thumb grazed over it, and it flicked away. She raised her fingers as though to trace the moon's shadows, only to notice her milky skin had a bruise-like patch of skin in lieu of the scab. She frowned, rubbed the painless discolouration, now focused on the welts across her palms. They pained little from the half-hearted punishment dealt by Mrs Embrey but more so, from clinging for her life in the well.

Mrs Embrey had questioned Eliza a dozen times that morning as to how she came to be soaked to the bone.

"Why do you let those girls treat you so?" Mrs Embrey had asked whilst kneading the life out of bread dough. Eliza shrugged, her attention on the floor powdered with flour. The kettle boiled. Mrs Embrey dusted her hands on her apron and busied herself making a pot of tea. Eliza had stood numb with cold and fear by the warmth of the kitchen hearth, listening to a bubbling pot and crackle of flames.

"Lass, are you listening to me?" Eliza jerked her attention from a curl of smoke that seemed to take its time to wind up the chimney. She nodded quickly and curtsied in reply. Mrs Embrey pursed her lips and huffed. "I didn't save you from your Ma selling you to the local bordello just to have you abused by those spoiled brats," She waddled over and passed Eliza a steaming brew. Mrs Embrey blew a weary sigh in Eliza's direction and dabbed sweat from her brow. "You give an old woman no choice when you refuse to speak the truth about what you've been up to, or speak at all, for that matter. If you tell me what happened and where my tartlets are, I'll spare you the switch." Mrs Embrey's wide eyes had implored Eliza; she'd given her every opportunity to speak of the well incident. Yet, despite the truth sitting in her throat like a barb, Eliza's words remained unspoken. She looked away from Mrs Embrey and twisted her fingers together. A short silence followed, broken only by the boiling and bubbling of pots, and the crunch of horse hooves and carriage wheels outside.

Mrs Embrey then slapped her tea towel down on the workbench. "Lord preserve me, Eliza!" She rustled for something under the bench. "Drink up that tea for your strength now," Mrs Embrey's voice was muffled as she had to kneel to look for what she was seeking. She groaned as she rose back up, cracking her spine back into place with a quick twist.

"You've got a voice, my love, you should use it as God intended." Her cheeks flushed with exertion as she placed a bundle of sticks bound with string upon the bench. Eliza felt shame as her beloved protector clutched the edge of the bench and breathed in and out slowly through pursed lips. A new sheen of sweat coated Mrs Embrey's brow. Her chins wobbled as she shook her head again and pointed the switch at Eliza.

"One day, mark my words, my dear, you'll speak up for yourself and by the blessings of the Lord or the Devil himself," She performed a breathless sign of the cross, "You'll need to if you want to see your next birthday. Those sisters will be the death of you! Now, hold out your hands."

With a tear in her eye, and her lips a firm, thin line, Mrs Embrey struck Eliza's hands just hard enough to satisfy the Lord and Lady that justice had been served.

Eliza felt no ill will for the punishment. She loved Mrs Embrey, or felt something warm inside her that she assumed must be love. It was a feeling that didn't hurt, didn't want to make her pick at her scars. Eliza stared at the moon, lost in chaotic thoughts until its light drenched the end of her bed. She shifted her feet under the quilt where the house cat, Agnes, curled like a foot warmer. She watched the rise and fall of her black fur with every purr-filled breath. Eliza was her favourite, as she gave Agnes leftovers whenever she could, and despite what Mrs Embrey would have anyone believe, she too was known to throw a little this and that out the kitchen door whenever Agnes mewed for a treat.

Eliza smiled sleepily, supposing that perhaps this creature was her friend. Agnes never harmed or threatened her, and was a comfort she could count on each night. As though knowing she was being admired, Agnes opened one eye and peered at Eliza through a small, green slit. She yawned, stretched out luxuriously, one paw extended, inviting Eliza in for a pat. Eliza smiled wider, and she sat up to reach for the cat. Just as her fingers ran across the soft fur, Agnes sat up, pupils dilated. Her body statue-still, the cat stared beyond Eliza's shoulder, her whiskers twitched. Her tail swished left and right, just as she did when on the hunt for prey.

Eliza followed the cat's gaze over her shoulder. Perhaps it was a horrid spider Agnes would make a midnight snack of. Eliza shivered as she peered with trepidation over her shoulder and sighed with relief; only the old wooden crucifix broke the bareness of the wall above her bedhead. Eliza's attention snapped back as Agnes leapt from the bed. Her claws snagged the quilt and dragged it to the floor. She circled at the door, growling and hissing, not her usual sweet mews to be let out. The cat bared her teeth towards the window and spun faster at the door. The curtains shifted slightly even though the window was shut.

Eliza reached to light her candle; unease chilled her skin. It was not where she left it, which was odd as the last thing she did before sleep was to snuff it out. She bit her lip, scanning the floor to see if it had somehow fallen from her bedside table. It was nowhere to be found. Her eyes roamed back to the door. The key was as she had left it, locked to the right so no one could have come in to take it. Eliza scratched her wrist as she watched Agnes paw at the crack of light under the door, hissing into the shadows to the right. Nerves fluttered in her belly. Eliza pressed on the dark patch of skin that had begun to burn. She chewed on her thumbnail until it formed a sharp edge, then sawed it across her skin until a new wound opened, a more comforting distraction. She squinted at the corner, had something moved? She pulled her knees up to her chest. Agnes began to howl; her hackles were up.

Not wanting the other servants to complain in the morning, Eliza slid her feet to the floor, eyes repeatedly flicking to the corner. Her toes curled back at the unseasonal cold of the boards. A shiver shook through her upper body, and she hugged warmth into herself. She reached for her shawl at the head of her bed; it too was not where she left it, but draped over the mirror above her washbasin. She was certain she hadn't left it there, but she quickly snatched it up, avoiding the oval reflection and let the cat out. She turned the key quickly to the right again.

Eliza shuddered against the door, her back pressed hard against it as she stared at the blackened fire grate that should still hold embers of warmth. She felt foolishly scared as she wished for the cat's return just to have another living body in her room, a room which suddenly felt strange and uninviting. She clutched the collar of her nightdress with one hand, her shawl with the other as though it would somehow protect her from whatever was getting under her skin.

Cold grasped her ankles. The hem of her nightdress fluttered. She peered down to see a wisp of white curl under the door and around her feet. It hung like a winter's frost, then evaporated. The floor outside creaked. The tick of the clock upstairs chimed three times. Eliza pressed her lips tight; a surge of anger prickled through her hair. The bruise on her wrist tingled more fiercely. She felt certain this was the sisters trying to frighten her. They'd done it before, leaving a frog in her bed just last month, on her birthday.

Her shawl slipped silently to the floor as her fists balled. Eliza rubbed the sting in her wrist against her side, but it didn't settle, merely smeared fresh redness onto the fabric. She glanced to her left again. The shadows seemed darker, thicker. Their reach seemed closer to her feet.

Eliza's teeth squeaked as she ground her jaw. Anger flushed her face whilst fear coiled in her belly. Master of neither feeling, Eliza turned towards the door, rested her forehead against it for a moment, then pressed her ear against its flaking paint. Another creak in the hallway. She thought she heard vague whispers, footsteps upstairs; yet the harder she listened, the quiet of her room became a more ominous companion. Her fingernails dug into her palms. She wished she had the bravery to stand up to the sisters. She immediately surmised they must have picked the lock, snuck into her room, and stolen her candlestick to leave her in the dark. Her skin crawled at the thought of them watching her in the vulnerability of sleep.

Ever so quietly, Eliza twisted the lock open and cracked her door ajar. She winced as it squeaked and held her breath before she peered through the gap down the hall. To the right, a dark recess bathed in the quivering light of a dying lantern. No one to be seen. Braver, she slipped her head around the door frame to the left and found no sign of anyone, just another long corridor with the servants' staircase at the end. The house was quiet.

Yet, despite shaking her head to clear it and wiggling her fingers in her ears, those distant whispers remained. With one last check for any sign of the sisters, Eliza quickly re-locked the door. She clutched her forehead; it was foggy with sleeplessness. The beginnings of an ache clawed behind her ears. She wasn't sure if she was relieved or not to find herself alone. She took another deep breath and concluded she must just be exhausted.

Eliza pushed away from the door, intent on re-lighting the fire, but stopped in the middle of the room. The bed linen was folded orderly upon her bed, her sleeping cap puffed up neatly, ready to wear on her pillow. Eliza's entire body jolted. She clutched for her shawl that was no longer around her shoulders. Her mouth dropped open, her thoughts ran wild, rewinding, trying to recall when she had done this? Was she dreaming? She pinched the back of her hand; it stung; she bit her lip, a trickle of blood spilled into her mouth; she was definitely awake. After a few moments of being glued to the spot, Eliza rationalised she must have picked it all up as she left the bed to let out Agnes; she did like to keep her room tidy.

Still, a shiver rattled through her as she rushed to the hearth, eager to get warmth and light back into the room. She plucked up a large lump of coal from a basket next to the hearth. It was cool and smooth. It stained her hand as dark as the strange new bruise inside her wrist. She struck her second-last match into a handful of kindling before dropping the coal into the ash, encouraging the birth of new embers. She stoked it into a satisfying flame. Her body relaxed as the gentle crackling interrupted the deafening quiet of the hour and the persistent mutterings she was trying to ignore. As she warmed her hands, telling herself she was clearly over-tired, the fire hissed and snuffed out as though doused with water. A curl of black smoke coiled anti-clockwise up the chimney. Eliza froze in place, just like the cat had, hands immobile, spread-eagled in front of the lifeless hearth.

A breath of cold rushed from the chimney; its bitterness doused any remaining bravado she had. An icy pain stabbed through her back; it enveloped her like a cloak. She was powdered in coal dust. Eliza coughed into her hand, her throat sore and dry as though a lump of coal was wedged in it. Wiping her mouth and face clean with the hem of her shift, she sniffed her nose clear, noticing her skin smelled like a Sunday roast; she grimaced and coughed again.

Eliza signed the cross over her chest twice, just to be safe, terrified of whatever ghost must certainly be hovering behind her. She fumbled for the small crucifix around her neck and pressed it to her lips. She stood, eyes shut and unsteady with the torrent of fear that invaded her. She turned around, ready with a prayer and an eye for the door to escape the entity that had most assuredly invaded her room.

There was nothing there. A bed, a chair and four corners of shadows. She quickly snatched her shawl from the floor and pulled it tight about her shoulders. A quivering sigh escaped her throat, her breath a white mist.

The window rattled. She tiptoed towards it, immediately confident the sash was open just a crack and the quite reasonable cause of the chill and ill-feeling. She couldn't refrain from a quick glance at the orderly bedclothes as she passed; however, the cause of that much more inexplicable.

Eliza's hands shook as she tugged the window latches looking for the source that snuffed her hearth and fluttered the curtains. The window was shut tight. Its handles were bitter with the frost of mid-winter when it was a balmy late spring. She sighed, tired and confused, hugged herself for comfort, and peered outside.

The moon was lower in the sky, morning neared, and a long workday loomed after such a poor night of sleeplessness. Eliza pressed her palm to the pane and wondered what the moon knew of the goings-on of the night. Was it an all-seeing queen of the dark, of creatures and things best left in children's fairy tales? The glass felt like ice. Eliza yanked her hand away from its burn, alarmed by the frosted handprint left behind. She jerked back further when the window shuddered again. Black feathers stuck on the glass as a bird slid to the ground. Her hand pressed against the cold glass again, the feathers flickered in the night's breeze. Her heavy eyes drew past a splatter of blood, out towards the shadows at the back of the garden. Questions about why a bird should be out at such an hour were pushed away as her attention was drawn across the perfect lawn, over the neat gravel path, up towards the hedgerow; a lovingly manicured evergreen hedge that defined the wilds of the Galdrewold forest from the civility of Norlane Hall.

Something moved, and with haste. A dark blur darted here and there across the lawn. Eyes narrowed,

Eliza sighed with relief to see it was Agnes pouncing across the vast greenness, leaping over the gardener's rake and under his barrow. The sleek cat disappeared under the hedgerow into the forest beyond the here and the there. Eliza bit her lip, worried momentarily about Agnes, but then rationalised the cat was after a rat or some other plump snack.

The moon's ambience did not seem to reach into the shades of the Galdrewold. It was as though an artist could only see fit to define the forest's entirety as a black smudge behind the colour and vibrancy of Norlane Hall. The forbidden forest lay hidden along with its mysteries beyond the hedgerow, dark and ominous like the stories told about it to scare little children.

A new and vague whisper erupted in the back of Eliza's mind, a husky sound, a beckoning that didn't so much scare her as it urged her to reach for the window latch again. An aching cold deepened under her skin, but a strange, comforting heat blossomed in her cheeks. A push and pull sensation, a need to both run towards and away from something all at once. Her heart raced a little faster, loud in her ears, heavy in her chest.

Mesmerised by the mystery of the world beyond the hedgerow, Eliza's eyes glazed over. She rested her hand once more on the arctic glass, eyes coming back into focus as her skin tingled and the tiny hairs on the back of her hand stood erect. She pulled her hand, but it seemed stuck. Her breaths quickened as she tried to ease her hand away, one finger at a time. The window frosted around the edges. Ice crystals spread towards her hand, delicate snowflake patterns of beauty that beheld terror in their mystery. Shadows crept closer from the corners, reached down from the ceiling, unencumbered by the moonlight. She signed the cross with her free hand, the other stuck fast.

Eliza grunted and wished a more powerful prayer, but no words came to mind in her panic. Something banged to her right. The crucifix had slipped from the wall and careened under her bed. She squealed. The air felt heavy on her shoulders, her mouth a barren desert. She licked her quivering lips, but moisture would not wet her tongue. Stuck and terrified as she was, she tried to calm herself. She drew a more controlled breath in and breathed out slowly. Eliza chastised herself, convinced she was dreaming again. Eyes squeezed tight, she wished herself awake. But the cold pain in her hand was real, and if she was taught anything, it was that you didn't feel pain in a dream.

Panic overcame sense and bravado. Eliza pulled her hand harder; the window rattled on the sashes. Her hand remained frozen to the glass. Her fingers burned until they became numb. She stretched out her right foot, hoping to hook the bedside table with her toes and drag it and its glass of water closer. She planned to pour it over her hand to release her skin. She wobbled on her left foot until she could just about reach the table leg. The table scraped a mere inch before she had to drop her leg back down as she nearly lost her footing. Eliza fell against the window ledge, a bruise sure to be deep on her elbow by morning.

After one more failed attempt at peeling her palm from the glass, she drew as much saliva as she could into her mouth, which was hard when parched with fear. Ready to lick her hand free, she stopped, spittle ready on the tip of her tongue. A sound vibrated the window pane. She watched, mouth agape, heart thudding heavily as the frosted shape of another hand materialised on the window, a twin to her own.

Eliza's insides burned hot, then twisted with cold. Her mind blurred as though afflicted by fever. The icy fingers elongated across the pane, growing before her eyes. They were not at all like her own small hand.

Long, thin digits, out of proportion to the palm, made their icy course until they looked like the claws of a bird. Sweat stung Eliza's eyes. She wiped them against her sleeve to clear her vision, the smell of terror pungent on her. She blinked the sting away, hoping the apparition would be gone. Yet there it remained, a strange, cloudy film, mere inches from her own hand. Eliza's hair fluttered forwards over her shoulder as though someone blew into her ear. The shadows verged onto the window frame. She gasped and squeezed her eyes closed; her entire body trembled. She didn't want to look behind, in front, anywhere. If she were to die, she'd rather it be quick and not see the devil that surely was haunting her. She gulped for breath; tears streamed hot down her cheeks as she waited to be killed where she stood. No death blow arrived.

The fluttering ceased, and her body calmed. Whilst her hand remained stuck, the cold stilled its grasp of her, her chin stopped quivering. She listened intently to her surroundings. All was still and silent. For a moment, she wondered again if the sisters were somehow responsible for her predicament. The thought of their perfectly happy faces crowned by perfectly curled hair dried Eliza's tears. The noxious terror ever-present in her belly curled into an altogether different feeling — rage. The heat of anger cloaked her. It fanned the strange whispers that serenaded her broken soul.

Eliza opened her eyes. The shadows had receded, and she stared at the strange handprint anew. Her loneliness dulled a little by the strange chorus in her head. Her wrist burned more intensely; she twisted it up as far as she could. Another scab had turned black. A thin black vein connected the dark, scaly patches. She touched the new spot, it was hard like bark, and the skin around it flaked away as more narrow black tributaries erupted up the course of her arm, like the lines of a map. Her brows met, intrigue overwhelmed fear. Her other wrist tingled anew; she turned it over to find it too besieged by this strange skin malady. Its burn wasn't uncomfortable; it was — comforting.

Eliza returned her attention to the ghostly hand. Its impression was smooth and lacking prints. She felt compelled to place her other hand upon it. Why? She could not say. She reached slowly; the cooing in her mind intensified as her palm moved closer. Her bloodied sleeve slipped down to her elbow, exposing the strange lines journeying up her arm.

The crispness of the air no longer penetrated to her core; it was now refreshing the heat that pulsed under her skin. She reached for the strange handprint, and the instant her skin touched its freezing silhouette, her other hand released, and she fell backwards onto the floor. Eliza scrambled backwards, grabbed her freed hand, her mouth dropped to find the lines, scabs, and callouses no longer present, just smooth, clear skin. A tingle settled in the palm, it circled her left wrist, and there it stayed.

Eliza shuffled to her knees; eyes fixed upon the window. A whooshing sound disturbed the intense silence. She crawled on hands and knees around the end of the bed to find the hearth re-ignited of its own volition into a full and hearty fire. Warmth filled the room, the smell of the charcoal comforting, yet she scuttled away as wisps of white smoke coiled from the flames towards her. Eliza staggered to her feet. Fear rose again, a bitter burn in her throat. She glanced outside as a means to escape, but she was struck still by the shadow beyond the hedgerow. The twists of smoke slithered up the wall, eked out through the tiny gaps around the window frame. They glistened like silver snakes as they twisted and turned across the lawn, all the way to the hedgerow, where they disappeared within it, just like Agnes. Something was out there, and it wanted Eliza's attention.

The latch wouldn't budge at first, but the whispers were insistent. The voices called a little louder when she thought again of hiding under the bed. They were a veritable opera when thoughts of the spiteful sisters crossed Eliza's mind again. Exhausted and frustrated, she grabbed the fire stoker, warmed by the crackling flames, and banged the latch three times until it opened with a squeak. She stopped, gripped the iron in her fist and turned her ear to the door, listening to hear if she'd awoken Mrs Embrey just two rooms down the hall.

Quiet reigned, other than the voices, soft once more, that sung between her ears. If she'd had a mother who was motherly, Eliza would have thought the voices warm and loving, but loving was not something she was familiar with. Mrs Embrey and Agnes bestowed upon her the most affection she had ever had. Yet, Eliza wasn't sure she could recognise real love, not until now, not until the choir in her mind that night.

She knotted her shawl in front of her chest and gave the hedgerow another glance, telling herself again she was probably just vividly dreaming, but her legs were straddled over the windowsill before she realised it, and within moments her feet ran through fresh cool grass, bare and free.

Eliza pulled up at the ancient wooden gate that led into the Galdrewold and leaned her hands onto her thighs, puffing hard. Peering over her shoulder, the expanse of lawn that led back to the house was filled with quiet and shadows. Nothing, human or otherwise was chasing her. Eliza sighed with relief and stepped onto the path that ran alongside the hedgerow. The softness of the grass had given way to a more uncomfortable prickle underfoot and she immediately wished she had shoes on. Besieged by intrigue, she ignored the discomfort of her feet and stepped closer to the hedgerow. The perfectly curated rose gardens mingled with a denser aroma of old leaves and earth. She swallowed a little harder, her eyes so wide they pained. Her body warmed a little more as her belly writhed with nervous excitement.

Eliza pulled on the circular handle. The gate jiggled, the wood creaked, the hinges groaned, but it was locked tight. Her brows furrowed. There was a large slot for a key she did not possess. She looked back to Norlane Hall; a grand home encrusted with a hundred-year-old vine that hid the gloom within. It was dark and silent, just one window aglow on the second storey with the light of someone moving about. If she was seen out here, what would happen? But that fear, that dreadful, every-day curl in her stomach was at that moment, overpowered by an enticement to go beyond the borders of servitude.

She took a step backwards, the stones still bit underfoot, but thrill dulled the sting. The hedgerow was vast in height. Eliza had heard the Norlane gardeners talk of its folklore age whilst they tended its precise square edges. It was a perfect evergreen beard around a perfect never-changing home. It was a line not to be crossed. A barrier that kept the civilised safe from the wilds outside, from things that weren't pretty and perfect, from that which needed to be buried and hidden away.

The hazy whispers notched louder. Eliza cocked her ear to the right; almost certain it uttered her name. Eliza twisted around to find no one behind her, only a milky moth fluttering towards the mesmerising glow of the moon. Her gaze followed its path until it disappeared beyond the hedgerow. Alone, the world around her silent, she only had the chorus in her mind to keep her company.

Eliza bit the back of her hand and picked a new wound into her wrist; the pain grounded her, put her in control of something. The deeper she scratched, the more insistent the murmurs. She listened to it, and her scratching ceased. The voices' gentle cadence took her pains away, folded up fear and extinguished it. She yielded to its gentleness, closed her eyes and drank deep of its calm. Eliza wondered if this was madness and the serenity of it felt a safer place to inhabit. The sweet lulling tempered everything with its intoxicating melody, absorbing her worries away.

Eliza opened her eyes and undid the knot of her shawl; its soft wool slid from her arms, letting the gentle night air taste her skin. Her toes clawed as she stepped gingerly across the gravel. She trailed her fingers through the leaves of the hedgerow. They were small, with a satisfying, glossy feel. She pushed her hand deeper into the loveliness, then yelped and yanked her hand quickly out. An unseen something pricked her middle finger. She sucked the blood away and searched for the culprit. A sting sung up the length of her finger and settled as an ache in her palm. She rubbed the tiny assault, trying to press the unwelcome pain away.

Less trusting of the voices that had wooed her outside, Eliza took a step back again. Instead, she studied the way the moonlight glittered across the top of the hedgerow. She could almost feel its weight, a power in its ambience. The mutterings were more excitable as blood trickled anew from her finger. She licked it away again, pressed on it with her thumb, intrigued to find the cause of the wound.

Eyes narrowed, she stooped, peering into the foliage. Something glinted within its depths. Eliza gently peeled a clutch of leaves apart, a twig snapped, and a cluster of leaves fell into her hand. The hedgerow rustled as though a shiver had run through it. She withdrew her hand, fingers curled around the leaves.

I'm sorry, she thought. Eliza placed the leaves gently on the ground, tucking them just under the hem of the hedgerow. Its shadow moved. She fell back onto her hip and scrambled away. A sickle-shaped darkness oozed across the sandstone crush. The shadow crooked around the leaves and withdrew, its spectral form pulled the plucked leaves back within the depths of the hedgerow.

Eliza pulled herself to her feet, ready to flee, but something held her there. Fear, intrigue, evil possession; utter madness? She bit her nails, looked in every direction. She dropped her hangnail to her wrist and picked a new wound. It oozed slowly. Fine black lines webbed out from it, just like before. Fear rose like a Phoenix and whipped her heart into a blistering pace. Eliza ran her fingers across newly blackened skin. Blood oozed from her pricked finger. She sucked it away, coppery and strangely satisfying as it coated her tongue. The feeling, all these strange feelings, shuddered through her until her head swirled. The greenery, the moonlight all smudged together.

The hedgerow bristled, pulling her from a near faint. The silent calm of the night held a new energy. It coated her skin, drew the hairs erect, pushed itself into her lungs. The smells beyond permeated through, heavy with rot and damp. Eliza stumbled back a step, but the voices weren't pleased, and they chorused at her. Their overture reverberated through her mind, louder again when she wobbled back another step.

The leaves quivered, garnering a sliver of her attention from the opera in her head. Wide-eyed, Eliza witnessed a hole yawn open in the thick of the leaves, just to the right of the gate. A dark recess where she had pricked her finger. Her hand pulsed more painfully, she rubbed it again, a groan deep in her chest with no relief to the ache. The dark river of lines inked towards her elbow, her milky skin now coarse and flaky. She pulled her sleeves to her wrist and retrieved her shawl, knotting it tight around her shoulders.

Something glinted in the moonlight from within the void of the hedgerow. Serenaded by the madness, Eliza obeyed the urgency of the voices. Her toes curled back as though something within her rebelled, but she traversed the path back towards the barrier between the known and unknown.

Eliza winced with each gravelly prick to her soles, yet hopeful the sensation might offer an anchor to reality. With each movement, normality felt further away, the cruelty of the sisters a mere dream. With the final step, the ensemble calmed into a repetitive melody as though pleased with her actions.

A rooster crowed; Eliza twitched out of her trance. It crowed again, and she twisted to see dawns' glow beyond the slate capping of Norlane Hall. She shivered, warmth tingled down her arms, leaving a fiery heat in her fingertips. Servants would soon rouse. She scanned for signs of movement in the house. Only the smoke from dying hearths curled away from the rooftop. All else was still.

Eliza returned her attention to the hedgerow, she picked again for comfort at her wrist. What lay beyond the ancient gate drew her thoughts immediately back to the strange happenings in her room. Eliza needed to know what was haunting her night, what was creeping under her skin. It would be impossible to exist in a world where both day and night were a terror.

Eliza stepped forwards until the leaves were a breath away. The hedgerow shivered again as though inviting her in. She never felt welcome, so she lay her palms against the soft leaves and gently pushed the greenery aside where the gap had opened.

Deep within the fabric of the foliage, a thorn as long as her thumb glistened with a drop of her blood. Eliza leaned in closer to the needle-sharp point. It twitched. She shuddered and clutched her pained hand over her heart. A smudge of red stained the buttons of her nightdress. Her pulse rushed in her temples and crashed against her palm. An itch coursed under her skin, up into her shoulder. She hesitantly peered in again.

The barb trembled. Leaves rustled around it. The air was still, yet the gate to her left rattled, its circular handle banged like a door knocker. Eliza was rigid with indecision. Held by the decadent harmony within her mind and the intrigue of the unknown, Eliza stared at the thorn whilst fear courted her as it so often did.

The dusk within the hedgerow leeched out as fingers of shadow drew the leaves further apart in invitation. Eliza's hand breached the fringe of greenery. The tip of the thorn quivered again as her hand closed in. A gush of wind whipped through the hedge. The thorn tip popped open; its tip curled back and sprayed something in Eliza's face. She jerked back, slapped at her cheeks, her hands slippery with a fine ash. She spat a fetid taste from her mouth, wiped her lips with the edge of her shawl. Her fingernails were back between her teeth. They clicked along the nail stubs, and she coughed some more.

Breathless, tremoring from within, she couldn't help but edge closer again, hand over her mouth and nose to silence words forever suppressed. Eliza dropped her hand to her side, her mouth agape with surprise. A flower had blossomed from the point of the thorn. She wrung her hands together, held them close to her chest. Her skin buzzed hot and cold.

The voices rose to a vibrato, filling her head with their rapturous excitement. Emboldened, Eliza leaned closer, leaves brushed against her cheeks. The damp of the forest beyond strong, the gentle whisper of a breeze not felt, rustled through its branches. In the darkness of night, in a hedge that never blossomed, were perfect layers of white petals. They yawned wider before her eyes until a full flower was formed. The stigma in its centre dark and shiny. With an unsteady hand, she gently tilted the blossom closer and sniffed.

Eliza coughed and wretched, letting the flower go. She covered her mouth and nose with her hand, glaring less admiringly at the strange bloom, feeling wronged by its rotten odour. Swallowing the sting from her throat, she noticed the stigma dripped fluid from its centre. A slit of dawn light struck the petals. The flower's tear was crimson. It streamed down the petals to drip into the shadows.

Touch it. The words were not so much formed in her mind as they were a feeling, as though her subconscious was telling her what to do. Eliza reached out despite herself; her fingertip dabbed the redness from the petals. She rubbed its slickness between thumb and finger. It tingled. The breach of her pricked skin invited it in, and the blood of the hedgerow flower seeped within her. Fire raged up her arm; it exploded through her body with the very next beat of her heart.

Breath was punched from her lungs. Eliza leaned forwards, desperately gasping to suck air back in. She grabbed her throat, the skin dry and crusty like her arm. Blood rushed to her face, her cheeks burned, the skin stung as it split, blood ran down her chin. Her pulse pounded in her temples, clouded her vision. Her face felt ready to explode. Rigidity struck through her limbs, and she fell back like a plank. Crickets stopped chirping; a veil of cloud cocooned the base of the waning moon, and there she lay, immovable, vulnerable, terrified.

Eliza's lungs eased, by a small measure, and she panted for breath, her rapid gasps loud in her ears. They obliterated the gentle whispers and left fear in its place. Her vision slowly cleared as air seeped back into her chest, yet her body remained paralysed. Assured this was death, Eliza relented to it and set her gaze upon the velvety sky, pinpricked with a million fading stars as they melted in dawn's light. Their attention weighed heavily upon her as she watched in a vacuous, frozen silence. She couldn't pull a prayer to mind; even her thoughts were muted. Instead, she felt pain. The ache in her hand burned stronger; it slithered deep inside.

Fire struck with each heartbeat, every inch of her alight. Each pulse a jolt, igniting her insides, whilst the cool soft grass cocooned her frozen form. She waited for death, but death too ignored her. For how long she lay there, she was unsure. Her breaths slowed, the burning waned, but haunted her like a second skin within, reminding her of its presence. One of her fingers twitched, the smell of smoke invaded her senses, the crackle of flames and screams raged in her head. Two fingers moved, then a toe. The voices returned, mewing at her, fanning the flame of resentment, a quiet resident of her thoughts. The purr of the voices became louder. Eliza's muscles released when something furry rubbed against her cheek.

She blinked, and feeling ebbed back into her body. Eliza drew large, relieving gulps of air. Agnes rubbed her wet nose against Eliza's cheek, her whiskers tickled reality back into Eliza's delirium. The cat licked her nose with her rough tongue. Strength returned to Eliza's legs.

Eliza's feet pounded through the cool morning dew. The cat bounded ahead, a guide out of this waking nightmare. Eliza scrambled into her room, slammed the window down, latched it tight and fell to the floor. She heaved for breath, scuttled away from dawn's glow into the shadows by her armoire. Every inch of her shivered.

So loud were her laboured breaths, Eliza did not hear the crackle at first, but the smell of roasting meat whipped her pulse impossibly faster. Eliza blinked the haze of sweat from her vision, let her shawl fall from her back. A new spring of sweat dampened her nightgown. Her nostrils flared as she sucked in the alarming smell. The hearth glowed as it should, but the air was insufferably hot. It burned down her throat, she could feel its heat deep in her chest. Eliza covered her mouth, it quieted her breaths, and that's when her eyes were drawn up towards the snap and crackle of fire.

Eliza flailed on the floor, pressed herself harder into the corner. She flinched as the wall burned her back. Her eyes were fixed upon flames that ran the length of the cornices, surrounding an apparition in the centre of the ceiling.

A figure, blackened to cinders, reposed in sleep or death. Its long hair and tarnished robes billowed against the plaster, fanned by the fire. Frozen in the shadows of her room, Eliza was unable to look away as the figure's eyes snapped open, the head turned, and glowing red orbs slid towards her.

A guttural scream followed Eliza as her knees and fingers clawed across the floor. Her room seemed so big, her limbs like jelly. Her body felt numb as her fingernails ripped across the floorboards. She heaved herself across the great expanse as though the air were made of molasses. Her room seemed to get bigger with each lunge forward. Heat pushed down from above, the voices sang in her head, chorusing her along until she hooked one hand on the bed frame.

All became silent, the heat dissipated, and the sweat that drenched her cooled her flesh into an uncontrollable shiver. Eliza pulled herself into the well-worn dip of her bed. She snatched the covers over her head and bit into her knuckles. Agnes snuggled under the covers with her, warm and purring as though all was well. Eliza held her breath and desperately sought a prayer.

The Hail Mary was on her mind, then the floorboards creaked. Her fingers gripped the sheets tighter again. She brought the linen to her mouth to muffle the tiniest of sounds. As prayer eluded her, she fumbled for the leather twine that held a crucifix about her neck. It was gone. Her despaired moan died within the linen that she bit harder into.

Her God had left her as he always seemed to do. *"Follow His commandments, and He will offer comfort,"* Mrs Embrey had taught her. Yet, Eliza could still feel the pinch to her ear when both she and her mother were thrown to the streets long ago. *"There's no room for you here. God's house is full,"* the vicar had hissed. There was no comfort from God that day, and there was little comfort from God in Norlane Hall. Her eyes burned. Anger fought fear. Fear squashed anger.

Despite it all, she couldn't help herself. Prayer was all she knew, even though not once had it reprieved her despair. Eliza rolled onto her knees, squeezed the image of the burning woman from her thoughts and prayed simply for sleep to take her away.

THREE

The morning sun glinted across a mirror that reflected a sallow complexion. Eliza poked at her cheeks; they were wan with the pallor of little sleep. Her fingers trailed the lines of her face, smoothed strands of chestnut hair behind her ears. Cracked lips umbrellaed the tremble of her chin. She ran her hands up and down her forearms; they were as they always were, pocked by her hidden picking. Her thumb smoothed over the scabs, dipped into the scars. She pulled her sleeves to cover her secret, and her attention settled back upon her eyes — glistening, bloodshot, one a little more hooded than the other. Eliza wondered if she were more a beauty, would her lot in life have been better? The thought was a lie to herself; women didn't fare well outside the upper classes. She dug a fresh wound just inside her elbow and sighed with morbid satisfaction. A scarred old crone is what she would become. Forgettable and not worth a second glance, and that she believed, would make her safe.

Chickens clucked noisily outside, which drew her attention from herself. This meant Mrs Embrey was collecting the eggs. Eliza splashed her face with some water and dressed quickly. She was already late for duty and wanted to busy herself with work, to forget the prior evening.

She had made good work of not looking towards the ceiling. She took a sharp breath, tucked her hair into a low bun and tilted her head up. The roof was as plain as expected, bar the cracks of time that spiderwebbed across it. Relief washed through her, a cool tingle that lasted only until she knelt to search for the crucifix that had fallen last evening. Her hands patted under the bed to no avail, she stood, hands-on-hips, surveying the floor. Eliza glanced to the nail it should have hung upon with the thought of how to replace it. She clutched her chest, the blood drained from her head, dizziness forced her to lean against the bed.

Jesus hung, inverted and blackened to soot; his sorrow destroyed. Despite fear catching every breath, Eliza made her way towards it. It was warm; her fingers came away black. Her heart hammered. She quickly righted the cross, but it no longer held its pious ambience. The wish that the prior evening had all been a dream dissipated. She backed away, eyes not leaving the damage, the evidence of her madness.

Eliza's palm stung again as she clung to the end of her bed. The cold of the wrought iron tempered the burn a little but only added to a new chill rising within. She shook her head, tried to clear her thoughts. She no longer felt comfort in Jesus' presence. Eliza plucked nervously at her lips; she ran her tongue over their hard edges, they stung. She steepled her tremoring fingers to her nose as her eyes glued to the charred crucifix. Could she have done all this in the daze of sleep?

Her hands returned to the bed frame, their tremor shook it, then she rattled it with frustration. It squeaked its complaint until she stopped, fearing a knock at the door. Tears weighed in her lashes. Was there no solace for her, not even in the privacy of her room?

Eliza moved back to her washstand, splashed the last of its water across the heat of her face. She tipped the mirror up, repulsed by the image, and peered again at the wall. Dream or not, she couldn't ignore this. The crucifix would have to be replaced before Mrs Embrey saw it. Reaching behind herself, Eliza lifted her apron from its hook and reversed out of her room, too scared to turn her back upon Jesus.

Eliza carried the cleaned breakfast dishes out of the scullery and set them aside for another maid to put away in the sideboard. She wiped her hands dry and collected the washing left for her at the back of the kitchen. Agnes weaved through her ankles along the rear path to the laundry room. The cat purred all the way; her comforting sounds eased the subtle shake in Eliza's limbs. Eliza breathed in the crisp morning air, the hint of gardenias upon it. She entered the laundry, thankful the copper was already boiling wildly. A snug flame had been set under it by Mrs Embrey at a much earlier hour. Eliza set down the wicker basket to stroke Agnes before the cat pounced effortlessly upon a pile of sheets under a steamed-up window. She curled into a snug ball and settled to sleep amongst the warmth.

Eliza began dropping the linens into the water. In the company of only the cat, she hummed to drown out her thoughts, to quell fear, to suppress anger. Eliza breathed in deep, her face relaxed, the hint of a smile tugged at her mouth. She relished the smell of the laundry; the hot starchy air was refreshing and clean. She liked the way it tickled her nostrils. It warmed her bones on the coldest of days. She enjoyed swirling the yellowed fabrics with the dolly stick, smoothed and softened by years of whirling amongst the starched fabrics.

The laundry was a place of solitude, a trusted companion. A sanctuary for Eliza where the old and worn, the used and the soiled entered in disarray and left fresh and white, clean and mended. She felt the same.

As she dropped boiling fabric into a cooler water bath, Eliza heard the ancient grandfather clock in the distance. Nine chimes. She groaned and dropped the stirring dolly, hoisted up the hem of her dress and rushed back to the house, grabbing her cleaning supplies along the way. She was late for her most loathed task.

Eliza's legs burned as she took the stairs two at a time. The bones in her hand cracked as she pulled on the balustrade to propel herself faster. As her boots sank into the floral carpet of the second story, she bent over, huffing and gasping for breath.

"What on earth are you doing?" Lady Norlane's voice shuddered through Eliza, and she looked up before she could stop herself. Their eyes met. Eliza dabbed the sweat from her face with the back of her hand, curtsied, she tried to look away, but felt frozen to the spot. Silence swung between them like a pendulum.

The heady toilet water Lady Norlane tended to overuse wafted about her; roses left in a vase a week too long. Lady Norlane pressed a hand over her bosom as though overcome by the sight of Eliza. Lamplight glinted off her diamond bracelet. She glared down over a thin, pointed nose. Lady Norlane grimaced.

Eliza swallowed back the lump of nerves, of nausea and fear, that constant coil of dread that dwelt within her. The grandfather clock ticked on downstairs, each strike of its hand too loud, each second dragged more terror to the surface.

Lady Norlane cleared her throat. "Does Mrs Embrey not teach you better? You are to meld with the walls, not look upon those above your station." Her nostrils flared as she twirled an emerald ring around a gloved finger.

Eliza stepped back; her gaze transfixed upon the ring. Worth more than she could earn in a lifetime, a twinge of anger competed with fear. Eliza opened her mouth, desperately wishing a word of apology, or any word for that matter, to emerge.

Lady Norlane held her hand up. "Do not even contemplate speaking in my presence. How dare you rush like a street urchin around my home and disturb my peace." Lady Norlane's lips pursed with disgust, tight like Agnes' backside. Eliza suppressed the sudden desire to laugh. For a moment, a little whisper in her ear enticed Eliza to let out the laugh, but she coughed away the giggle caught in her throat. Her insides tingled with the burn of the previous night, and it gave her a strange comfort.

Lady Norlane snapped her out of her impolite stare. She clicked her fingers in Eliza's face. "Get on with your duties." She waved Eliza away and turned to a mirror that hung nearby, adjusted her hair, tucked in an errant curl and smiled at her own reflection. She seemed shocked to look down upon Eliza again. "You're still here? Shall I call upon Lord Norlane to deal with you?"

Humour and the ghostly whispers dissipated quickly as Lady Norlane's words almost knocked Eliza back down the stairs. Eliza's hands fidgeted in the deep pockets of her apron, a loose thread coiled around her index finger, and she pulled at it. The air of the second floor felt heavy and old, harder to draw in. She could smell dust and old candles. She lowered her head, curtsied deeply, hoping for a reprieve. She studied the yellow and pink flowers threading through the red of the carpet, so soft underfoot, too scared to look up.

A baby cried. Lady Norlane sighed laboriously. "Nanny? See to my son immediately!" A door opened; Eliza peered through her lashes to see an old woman scuttle across the hall behind Lady Norlane. Eliza straightened from her curtsy slowly now that Lady Norlane's scowl fell elsewhere. "Why does that child never quiet?" Lady Norlane muttered to herself.

The crying settled. The Nanny limped back across the hallway and into the sanctuary of her own room. A sharp sting to Eliza's cheek called her attention back.

"Why have you not disappeared?" Lady Norlane readjusted the ring that had cracked over Eliza's cheek. She felt blood drip down her skin. Crimson spotted her clean apron as she dabbed her raw face.

With a new look of disgust, Lady Norlane moved towards the stairs, stopped and looked back over her shoulder at Eliza. "If you look upon me again, child, if I so much as notice your presence, even hear you draw a breath, you will be back to whatever cesspit it is you came from!" She flicked an exotic fan open and fluttered it a few times to settle the blossom of rage across her face.

Eliza's eyes burned. Her skin felt alight, her guts like jelly. She imagined Lady Norlane falling down the stairs, a crumpled knot, the fan wedged down her throat. The voices giggled; they liked her thoughts.

She had impressed them, and that eased the fear; settled her stomach. Eliza dabbed more blood from her cheek, lifted a finger to pick at her wound, but stopped herself. Instead, she backed up until her hip banged a small side table, precariously wobbling a vase that sat upon it. She quickly steadied the valuable yet ugly porcelain. The Lady tutted at her one last time before disappearing down the staircase with a dramatic swish of her dress.

Eliza stood a few moments longer, listening to the ticking of the clock. Every tick, every tock, felt like another slap. Eliza's hands balled inside her pockets; she was tired of fear being her master, sick of it commanding her pain, of pushing her to the brink.

The ever-unsettled babe screamed again, drawing her away from self-indulgent worries. Nanny scuttled back across the hall, muttering to herself. Eliza wondered what this child would be like. Would he, too, be as cruel as his family? As though on cue, the sisters bickering screeches migrated up the staircase. Her concerns about the baby faded. Eliza moved in brisk automation towards the bedrooms, an innate reflex to avoid her tormentors.

Margaret's room was first. Eliza tidied the clothes left askew on the floor, picked up two quills and paper beneath a small rosewood writing bureau. She paused over an unfinished letter. Her fingers trailed the looping sweeps of ink. They were harder to read than the print of the bible. This was how Mrs Embrey had taught her to read by candlelight, with warm milk and honey in the evenings. The paper crinkled in Eliza's hand, then her heart fluttered. The blush of something other than anger heated her cheeks.

The word *love* repeated across the page quite liberally. Horse hooves ground on the gravel outside. She glanced to the window, peered down and saw the edge of a carriage slip away through the front gates. She imagined being on that carriage with a secret love. Sighing, Eliza placed the paper neatly upon the bureau, the quills in their stand next to the inkwell.

The sisters' voices carried upstairs, in argument as usual. Eliza jolted back from her moment of serenity. She knocked the ink well over as she reached for her cleaning bucket. A wave of dizziness swept her as she watched the ink spill across the love letter. Footsteps pounded on the stairs. She panicked; her hands blackened as she tried to dab the blots from the letter.

Her heart was in her throat, the words obliterated as the ink seeped through the paper's fibres. Footsteps rose and fell on the stairs, arguing continued. Eliza hastily smoothed out the ruined letter and shoved it behind the bureau.

Eliza scrubbed her hands as clean as possible, smoothing their tremble away as she slipped them under the mattress and tugged crisp bedlinen into perfect neatness. Her attention wandered to the bureau multiple times. Margaret would know it was missing. She hastened her cleaning, needing to get out as quickly as she could. Eliza fell to her knees and reached for the chamber pot underneath the bed. Suppressing the urge to vomit, she held her breath and slid it out carefully so as not to spill. It sloshed half-full. Eliza turned her head to the side, gasped in a fresh breath, held it a moment, then exhaled. Still, bile hit the back of her throat at the sight. Gathering up her dress, she was about to stand when the door banged open. Margaret strode in; delight brightened her eyes when she saw Eliza kneeling by the vile pot.

Margaret laughed. "Just where you belong, amongst the shit." She sauntered towards Eliza; arms clasped behind her back. "You stink like the shit I leave for you." Her smile widened as Eliza shrunk back from her.

"Do you realise how disgusting you are?" Margaret leaned in a little and sniffed, her perfect hair bounced over her shoulders. Margaret screwed up her face and coughed behind her hand. "Definitely you, not the pot!" Eliza winced; her fingers tingled as they curled around the floral handle of the pot.

Margaret wandered towards the bureau. Eliza's vision blurred as Margaret ran a finger across the desk. "Hmm, dusty." She glared back at Eliza. Margaret's hip nudged the writing desk as she edged to the right to primp herself in a mirror. The letter slid from behind the bureau. Eliza grabbed the edge of the bed, nearly dropped the chamber pot. She reached for a rag, forced herself up and dashed to the bureau, dusting hurriedly as Margaret admired herself. Eliza worked her way over the top, around the edges and down the turned wood legs. She snatched up the letter as Margaret pouted at her own reflection, pinched colour into her cheeks and blew a kiss to herself. Eliza was about to slip the paper into her pocket when Margaret's head snapped around.

"What have you got there?" She snatched the paper from Eliza, her eyes narrowed. Margaret glared at Eliza. "Reading someone's private correspondence?" A smug smile softened Margaret's stare. "How utterly uncivilised." Eliza grasped the edge of the bureau, pulled herself up and leaned her hip into it for support. Margaret slipped her fingers into the folds and opened the letter. Her eyes widened as she ran her fingers over the paper. She then hugged it to her chest.

Smiling more broadly, Margaret waved the letter in Eliza's face. "I bet you wish you had a love to write about," She glanced at Eliza's hands. "But those such as you aren't fit for such sophisticated pursuits." Margaret dropped the letter casually upon the bureau and returned to her own reflection.

Eliza's nails dug into the desk. The letter was intact. The neat script untouched by the ink she had spilled. Voices burst into her scattered thoughts. The letter fluttered of its own volition, unseen by Margaret. Eliza backed away, unsure if she was relieved or terrified, or both. She jolted again as Margaret snapped at her. "Well, get on with your work. And get out of my room."

Eliza dropped back to the floor and reached for the chamber pot again. The soft coo in her ears calmed the race of her pulse, but her skin felt like ice down her neck. Margaret was muttering to herself, so Eliza focused on that to pull herself towards some sense of reality.

"Nearly seventeen, I'll be out of here soon. A lady of my own manor." She giggled, glancing over her shoulder at Eliza. "And you, if you're lucky, will work here until your old bones turn to dust."

Eliza wanted to laugh at Margaret, to scream, to throw the stagnant waste in her face. She wanted to run as far as she could from the voices, this house, but Eliza clutched the stinking pot a little harder. She kept her thoughts to herself, words always suppressed, desires never realised. She just stared at the brown slosh, trying to ignore the whispers and the shake of her body.

Margaret's dainty shoe tips entered the periphery of Eliza's vision. One shoe flicked forward, and the contents of the pot spilled onto both the carpet and Eliza. It was still warm as it seeped through to Eliza's skin.

"You'll want to clean that up before Mother finds out. She had that carpet imported at great expense, you know. I'm sure I won't have to tell on you if you promise to bring more tartlets today, you know, for our adventure into the forest. Oh, and of course you will get the key from what's his name…Mr Blythe, I think? You're the help, you know, the butler? He has the only one that will open the gate." Her head tilted to the side, awaiting a response.

The voices roared. Eliza's ears burned as they took over her thoughts. Her cheeks prickled as she imagined pushing Margaret's face into the pot, making her drown in her own excrement. The voices scoured through Eliza's veins, fluttered through each beat of her heart, slapped down fear. Eliza's knuckles whitened around the handle.

Footsteps pounded outside. The door swung open, the letter lifted on its breeze and fluttered across the room to land upon the urine-soaked rug. "Ugh!" Margaret snatched it up by a corner; the words bled away. She stomped over to the door. "Sybilla! Where are you? I know that was you!" She slammed the door shut and came back to Eliza; her face flustered as she let the letter fall on the moist patch of carpet.

"Get rid of that too. Now hurry up and get out; I wish to be alone." Margaret snapped.

The voices laughed, and Eliza felt less alone than she ever had. The rise of anger's intensity stomped on fear. She yanked a cleaning rag from her apron pocket, scrunched it so tight the bones in her hand cracked. She began to sop up the mess.

Margaret pointed the toe of her shoe, directing Eliza's cloth. "You missed a spot." She hovered too close; Eliza scrubbed a little quicker, her teeth ground until her jaw ached.

Margaret sighed. "I know you don't like to speak." Eliza glanced up. "Keep going." She flicked a hand at Eliza. "Are you mute or just plain stupid? Actually, I don't really care, nor do I know why I bother giving a thought to you." Eliza kept scrubbing. The whispers scratched more intensely in the back of her mind. She had the urge to reach out and yank Margaret's feet from under her. A hidden smile released the tension in Eliza's face.

"Are you listening to me?" Margaret stamped her foot down on the edge of Eliza's cloth. "Answer me, you stupid girl!"

Eliza froze. Filthy moisture squelched up between her knuckles. The murmurings were louder than Margaret's insufferable snapping. Eliza reached into her thoughts and welcomed their comfort. What was real or not real was of no consequence. She needed solace, and Eliza thanked her insanity for the reprieve.

Margaret's shoe tapped the pot completely over. "Woops!"

Eliza dipped the rag back into her bucket of water and squeezed out the putrid waste. She returned to sopping up the brown stain, wishing she could hush Margaret by stuffing the rag down her throat. The whispers laughed again.

"I can't stand this stink a moment longer." Margaret's shoes clicked on the floorboards as she made her way back to the mirror. "I'll expect you ready with the key and tartlets when the clock strikes one." She smiled at her own reflection again. "Mother will be sewing by then, and Father is off to see the magistrate in town. Her heels squeaked as she spun around. Eliza watched her through her lashes; the voices prodded for her attention whilst Margaret demanded it.

"Father will be gone all afternoon." Margaret's shoes silenced over the carpet and were once more near the stinking stain. "Someone is to be hanged, and he's a witness!" She giggled. "Wouldn't Annabelle just love it?"

The sounds of her infant brother's cries seeped through the walls, halting Margaret's laughter. "Ugh!" she stamped her foot. Margaret screeched towards the wall. "Calm that thing down, or I'll smother it myself!" She stomped away. The door slammed, and Eliza let out a sigh of relief. She finished as quickly as possible, dashed to the laundry to clean herself up and change her dress.

All too quickly, Eliza stood outside Annabelle's room. The dark wooden door was knotted with whorls under a perfect varnish, much like Annabelle. Eliza closed her eyes, took a deep breath and twisted the shiny handle. The door creaked; she thought of ponies and cakes and all things pleasant, then entered.

Annabelle's room was charged with an energy that set Eliza's nerves on edge. Eliza held onto the murmuring thread in her mind, clinging for succour as she stepped through the ungodly mess.

Just three years younger than Margaret, Annabelle retained furnishings more suited to that of a small child. A delicate white bed canopied with soft fabrics dominated the centre of a grand space. Childish playthings littered the room, but none were that which Eliza would ever have desired.

Heavy window drapes were strung with porcelain dolls hanging by their necks with the prettiest of ribbons. All dismembered in various states of torment. Eliza's skin crawled every single day that she traversed this den of horror. Her boot knocked a loose head. It rolled away, cracking in two against the far wall. Eliza shuddered. She held her bucket a little closer to her body and turned away only to come face to face with a new doll that hung from the bed canopy. A blue-ribbon around its neck, its face scorched, a crack split the forehead. Another lay naked and spread-eagled in a doll bed with its eyes plucked out. Its mouth was stuffed with dried mud. Eliza quickly threw a spare cloth across its face.

Others were intact, lined up in their pretty dresses against the wall under the window, yet to meet Annabelle's deranged attention. Eliza felt compelled to hide them, as though the dolls could feel the hatred that was dealt them. She refrained for the sake of her own well-being, only picking up their bits and pieces to take out to the garbage.

Eliza put her bucket down and picked up one of the newer dolls. She held it gently in her arms. She wound her little finger through the soft brown ringlets, brushed her fingers across the cool porcelain cheeks. It wore a pink dress trimmed with lace. Eliza brought the doll up to her chest, her head cuddled into it. It smelled of fresh paint and teacups. She held a secret wish it could have been hers. Just one pretty thing, one part of her not broken. A screech outside spoiled the moment, and she swapped the doll for her cleaning bucket once more. Eliza wandered to the window and pulled the curtains aside, careful to stay concealed as she squinted through the morning sunlight.

Eliza dropped her bucket noisily on the floor, its clean water sloshed onto the floorboards. Annabelle chased Agnes with a large stick. The cat bound under a clutch of bushes, then through the rose garden. Annabelle screamed with delight; a rainbow of hangman's ribbons dangled from her other hand. Eliza's fingers clenched the drapes, catching in the lace curtains behind. Her skin felt too hot. The voices screamed. She clutched her ears as tears weighed in her lashes. Eliza watched helplessly as Agnes ran for her life from Annabelle, along a path and finally up a magnolia tree to safety. Eliza sighed with relief.

Annabelle's shoulders slumped in disappointment. Eliza wiped away her tears and imagined it was Annabelle hanging from the tree. She shook her head, clearing the thought and her private chorus of encouragement.

Her fingers clutched tighter to the drapes as she spied on Annabelle waiting under the tree for Agnes. The girl dropped the stick and twisted a strangling ribbon between her hands and shouted something up into the foliage before kicking the trunk and walking away. As Annabelle calmly tied a ribbon through her hair, Eliza's grip relinquished the drapes, blood seeped back into her fingers. Backing away from the window, tension eased from Eliza's limbs as she retrieved her bucket and mopped up the spill. Her attention was once more caught by all the little bodies swinging here and there. She quickly pulled the bed linens into order, leaving the dusting for another day, and left.

Eliza crossed the hallway and entered Sybilla's room, closing the door behind her. Her shoulders slumped; she leaned against the door and breathed deep. Despite the cruelty of Sybilla, Eliza found this room the least offensive. Sybilla was rarely present, which was a small blessing.

Eliza plucked up the linens twisted into a nest by the hearth. Sybilla insisted upon sleeping on the floor, despite her mother's protestations. Eliza shook everything out and smoothed the bed back to a state of orderliness, and as usual, ignored the expressionless stare of the cherubic faces carved into the bed head as she fluffed the pillows.

Eliza then retrieved the books, writing quill and a new tapestry that Sybilla had dumped into a corner of the room. The writing bureau was closed, its ornate black and giltwood scratched; a broken ink well stained the floor underneath. A chair lay upside down by the washstand. Eliza couldn't imagine what would become of Sybilla in a year or two when the Lady and Lord looked to marry her off. She pitied the poor gentleman.

Eliza dusted the window, wiped down the washstand and bowl, all devoid of a frill or flower.

Even the floors she swept were bare wood, for Sybilla insisted she hated carpets. The room felt empty, exactly the way Sybilla's dark eyes looked each time she punched Eliza in the gut.

As Eliza packed up her supplies, she remembered the spilled ink and rushed back to the bureau. The hard bristles of her scrubbing brush circled quickly over the black fluid, but it was stubborn and a dark stain remained, so she positioned the chair over it and replaced the inkwell into its niche. Fatigue forced a sigh from her chest and she knelt, the prior evening's lack of rest already upon her. Eliza wondered how long she could just sit there, avoiding the rest of the day?

The clock in the room next door began to strike; she had no time to hide and retreat from reality. As she pushed up, Eliza heard the door creak. Fearing Sybilla had snuck up on her, she jumped to her feet, backed into the wall, bucket and stinking chamber pot protective in front of her. The door was shut, the room empty.

Eliza shook her head; she was clearly exhausted. She leaned a moment longer against the wall, a headache creeping up the base of her skull. She pressed her fingers on either side of her temples and massaged little circles.

With the clock still chiming midday, she made her way back to the door when she spied an errant cleaning cloth she had dropped by the bed. Her knees clicked as she knelt to pick it up. She wasn't sure if it was her own weary groans, but she thought she heard the same creaking sound again. She scrambled back to her feet, face to face with one of the cherubs on the headboard, its face broad with a static smile. Moss bristled between the lips where teeth should have been. Mouth agape, Eliza rubbed her eyes and looked again. The cherub was once more expressionless. She reached for her crucifix, which was no longer around her neck. Instead, she quickly crossed herself and hesitantly reached for the cherub. The wood was smooth, cool, and fit snug in her palm. Something moved against her skin. She pulled her hand away and yelped. The cherubic face stared at her in a petrified scream, green bearded its mouth once more. She fell backwards, spread-eagled on the floor. Eliza slipped in panic, knocked over the contents of the chamber pot. She scrambled through the mess, pulled herself up and ran. She hit the door but couldn't work the handle. She peered back, assured that Satan himself was behind her. The cherubic face was again expressionless, clean and glossy, as it always was. Something creaked again, the room unchanged. She turned back to the door, reached for the handle. It was hot, she jerked back. The handle glowed as red as a farrier's iron. The windows rattled; wind rushed through the unopened panes. The drapes fluttered like spectres. Eliza spun; her mind giddy. The floor creaked behind her, in front of her, the cherubs glared on, emotionless. Eliza pressed her hands to her head and screamed into her thoughts *Stop!* And all went still. The door clicked open. She ran.

Eliza hid in the laundry. She rocked herself in a corner, near the purrs of Agnes, who had found solace in there as well. She rubbed the ache in the base of her neck, squeezed her eyes shut to rid the cherubs, creaks and burning things from her thoughts. It had to be exhaustion. She mulled the thought over and over until her belly growled. She felt the rumblings, the pops and gurgles under her hand and nodded to herself. Her mind eased a little. She was clearly deranged from lack of sleep and breakfast. Yet, as she leaned closer to the boiling copper, no heat or steam could warm away the chill in her bones. She hugged her body still, trying to calm herself as the reverberations of the grandfather clock struck the luncheon hour.

Eliza changed her soiled clothes once more. An ill-fitting dress was conveniently hanging in the back of the laundry. She left Agnes purring upon the linens, wishing she could curl up and do the same. Margaret's threats and demands invaded Eliza's thoughts. Eliza had no choice but to go and fetch the tartlets and key to the gate of the hedgerow; she dared not think of the consequences of not doing so. The voices whispered distantly, daring her to do as she pleased. Temptation to disobey begged her to listen; fear hurried her footsteps along the path away from the laundry's solace and back to the house.

She curled her fists and shook her head to rid unwelcome thoughts. A fiery heat enveloped her. A high-pitched screech burdened her ears; louder every moment that she urged the voices to hush. She stopped outside the kitchen door and pumped a little water to quench her dry mouth as well as to splash sense into herself. Every mouthful of water, however, seemed harder to swallow than the last. Water dribbled from the corners of her mouth, and when she wiped it away, her lips felt a little numb. Her tongue swept over them to find them rougher than before. Eliza hastened back through the kitchen, prodding at the strange sensation. Her face tingled with unabated heat; her thoughts chaotic. The voices had died away. She felt feverish; her body shivered every few seconds. Her hand pressed against a hollow loneliness in the pit of her stomach. This house, the hedgerow, the Norlane family, they all seeped under her skin, and she was sure it would kill her.

Eliza crossed the kitchen and tiptoed upstairs. She peered out into the main hall. Nanny hobbled up and down the parquetry, trying to calm the whimpers of the son. Eliza headed back down through the kitchen and found Mrs Embrey waddling in with the silverware to polish for the evening meal. "Well, get on with you then. Help an old lady out." She inclined her head towards a board of sandwiches that needed plating.

Setting out luncheon took the focus of the strange feelings scraping under her skin. Eliza busied herself, one eye on the corridor towards the butler's office, the other on the fresh tartlets Mrs Embrey had just pulled from the cooker. Their jammy sweetness made Eliza's mouth water. Mrs Embrey covered them with a clean linen cloth and set them to cool by the window.

"What are you gawking at? Hurry up with you," Mrs Embrey waved Eliza on. The cook, in a constant state of fluster, stopped and turned back to Eliza. "Where in the Lord's name is your cap?" Her eyes narrowed. "And what on earth are you wearing, girl? That looks fit to drape my ample backside!" Mrs Embrey pursed her mouth, shook her head, and turned away before she could see Eliza bloom with embarrassment.

While the Mrs Embrey was tinkering in the larder, Eliza quickly wrapped three warm tartlets into a fresh linen cloth and slotted them into her pocket just as Mrs Embrey wandered back in. "Here then," she fluffed out a spare cap and pulled it down over Eliza's bare head, wandered back to the counter and pulled a warm tartlet out. "Come then, you missed breakfast, eat up." Eliza didn't need to be asked twice. The sticky tartlet was in her mouth, rolling over her tongue. She sighed with a moment of contentment then carefully dabbed the crumbs from her pained lips.

Mrs Embrey had watched her closely as she ate, her arms crossed and her face pinched in concentration. "Hmm…what is this then?" Mrs Embrey ran her thumb across Eliza's mouth, her face scrunched with worry. She held Eliza's face between thumb and forefinger. She huffed and wandered back into the larder, emerging soon after with a small pot. She pulled the cork lid away and scrapped an unguent onto her fingers. She held Eliza's face still and smoothed it across Eliza's lips. Mrs Embrey then pushed Eliza's sleeves back and dabbed the wounds on her wrists. Shame tinted the pallor of Eliza's face.

"You must stop this, Eliza. Those girls are not worth such pain. Don't indulge them, my dear." Mrs Embrey gently pulled the sleeves back into place and held Eliza by the shoulders. She tilted Eliza's chin up to see her face. The cook's watery eyes stared deep into Eliza's. Eliza dropped her head again, unable to meet them. They stood for a moment before Mrs Embrey squeezed Eliza's shoulders then picked up the laden platter.

"Well, get on with you then, girl! Ring the luncheon bell!" Mrs Embrey said impatiently, her cheeks red, the sweat of hard work yellowed her cap. "Once luncheon is underway, you can sit yourself in the scullery and polish the Lord's shoes before we get started with the silverware. That should keep you away from those dreaded girls for a while." This was most convenient for Eliza as the scullery was only a hair's breadth away from Mr Blythe's office. If she was to find this gate key, it would surely be there.

Eliza pulled the brass chain; it chimed upstairs and initiated a rush of activity around the kitchen. As the other servants came and went, Eliza kept herself occupied passing out platters to the servers, one eye towards Mr Blythe's office, her mind otherwise worried about spectres, dark forests and death.

Waiting for the hustle and bustle to settle, she scrubbed a pot, wrapped a cooled loaf of bread and placed it in the larder whilst she waited for Mrs Embrey to predictably lose her patience with the slow pace of the servers at the base of the main staircase. Eliza smiled whilst Mrs Embrey snapped impatiently about the horror of a hot meal gone cold.

Lord Norlane's gruff voice carried downstairs as he yelled for more brandy. Eliza stopped wiping down the workbench and wandered to the window. Despite its grandeur, Norlane Hall had thin walls; little was a secret. Lady Norlane knew very well of the Lord's unwelcome visitations to Eliza's room at night. He was fat and loud, a disgusting smelly beast who took no measure to hide his vile behaviour. Eliza's nails dug into her wrist.

All the hurts and pain of her life haunted every moment, following her in thought and sensation. The words that stung, the punches from Sybilla, the awful burn between her legs from the Lord's probing fingers. She never understood why she felt shame, as though she were to blame for all these assaults. Shame and fear flooded each void that wasn't crammed with chores. Her eyes glazed, she filtered out Lord Norlane's complaints and stared out the kitchen window towards the hedgerow, wondering on mysteries of the Galdrewold.

For a moment, she thought of running deep into what lay beyond the greenery, far from the horrors of Norlane Hall. Perhaps it wouldn't be any worse. Her eyes narrowed as she focused intently upon the hedge, and the voices tapped back into her thoughts. They whispered soft nothings; all the pains were forgotten. She could smell fresh blossoms, the mineral tang of a bubbling brook, feel the gentle embrace of a spring breeze rush across her hot skin. Her hand fell away from her wrist, and she took a step towards the back door out to the garden.

Then Annabelle screeched, and it tore Eliza away from the gentleness that was calling. She snapped back to the smells and heat of the kitchen. Annabelle's tantrum reverberated through the walls. Eliza held her breath and could just hear her calling Mrs Embrey a fat old witch. Her teeth ground as she heard hushed words, perhaps a scolding, because this was followed by the familiar sound of feet stomping up the grand staircase and a door slamming.

Eliza felt something cool in her hand. Her attention fell to a carving knife she hadn't realised she had picked up. It was wet with pheasant juices. She lifted it up, watched the red-tinged fluid drip from its blade and imagined plunging it into the sisters, one by one. A new rush of heat hit her face; her heart thundered. Her vision clouded. She blinked hard, crossed herself, but her eyes remained a moment longer on the sun's glint along the length of steel before she threw it onto the bench.

Eliza leaned into the bench and squeezed her eyes tight. She opened them and turned away before she could be entranced by the blade again. With the distraction of a childish tantrum upstairs, the kitchen and servants quarters were empty. Footsteps padded hastily on the first floor. Mrs Embrey and Mr Blythe would be trying to keep a sense of civility and decorum in the dining room. This was her chance.

Eliza dried her hands on a rag and stuck her head out the door to ensure the corridor was clear. The staircase was empty. She tip-toed quickly towards Mr Blythe's office. She felt sure that if she was caught, this would see the end of her employment and a guaranteed bed in a ditch on the streets for her. However, the fear of the sisters' threats was still a greater risk than sneaking in to borrow a key.

Eliza pictured the hedgerow as her hand rested on the cold brass handle. She imagined the tranquillity of a forest, held her breath and pressed her ear to the door. She was almost sure that Mr Blythe was in the dining room but not entirely certain for the commotion had settled, and there was quiet once more. Only the tick-tock of the grandfather clock cut through a pressing silence.

Do it! The whisper made her flinch; her hand jerked back from the handle as though it had burned her. She turned it over, wriggled her fingers. A welt ran from the pricked finger to her wrist. She grabbed it with her other to quell the return of the fire under her skin. *Take the key*, the breathy voice was right behind her; she felt its heat in her ear. Eliza spun around. She was alone in the corridor.

Come to us, the melodic lull nestled snuggly within her mind. Her hands rolled over and over, she peered back and forth up the corridor, hoping for a rational explanation. Alone, unbalanced by a tremor, she backed up against the opposite wall, convinced she was entirely mad. Hands pressed against the wall for support, she closed her eyes, tried to quell her rapid breaths. The words blended into nothingness, a soft tune that calmed as it sang. These imaginings were frightening yet somehow comforting. They drew out that new and strange feeling of not being so alone in the world. Eliza peered heavenwards. Perhaps she might have a guardian angel. At that thought, a warmth spread from within her chest. It dampened fear and let her hand fall away just as her thumb reached across to search for her scars.

Eliza moved back to the door and grasped the handle again, her fingers still quivered, but it was a new feeling altogether that made them tremble. The sensation tugged a smile from her. She turned the handle to the right before she could change her mind.

Like many rooms in Norlane Hall, the tick of a clock beat rhythmically in Mr Blythe's office, the heartbeat of the house. Eliza scanned the room quickly, hunched over and tip-toed as though this might lessen her chances of discovery.

A perfectly tidy desk dominated the small room. Grandly placed upon it were an ink well and white-plumed quill. A large leatherbound ledger sat proudly on it. A chair occupied either side of the desk with a wooden coat stand laden with heavy cloaks tucked against the wall. A walking cane leaned next to it.

She moved quickly, pulling at the locked drawers of the desk, sunk her hands into the deep pockets of the cloaks. Anxiety dampened her shirt collar as the tick of the clock made her all too aware of time passing. The delicate tartlets banged against her leg in her apron pocket as she hurried. She imagined the beating she would get if she turned up without the key and crumbled tartlets.

Eliza froze momentarily as voices echoed up the corridor. Her mouth dried as she smothered it, yet the air rushing from her nose seemed as loud as a locomotive. The clock struck a quarter to the hour; she shuddered with each lost minute. Footsteps thudded on the stairs. Up or down, she couldn't be sure. She looked under the desk for a place to hide. Panic pounded in her temples. The footsteps clicked closer; she heard Mr Blythe's voice just outside the door. She couldn't fit under the desk without scrunching into a tight ball, and that would surely destroy the tartlets.

Breaths came too fast, her vision clouded. Her whole body shook. She looked to the window as a means of escape, but it would surely creak when opened. She dashed to it anyway and tugged at the latches. Her sweaty palms slipped at first. She ran them down her dress, took hold again, and the window slid up; a relieved sigh rushed from her chest. As Eliza scrunched up her skirts, about to cock a leg over the ledge, a gush of wind blew through the opening. The gas lamps on the far wall flickered. The breeze rattled the coat stand, causing the walking cane to topple to the ground with a dull thud. Eliza nearly fainted. She braced herself against the window ledge, one hand over her racing heart, one across her mouth. The door remained closed, the voices outside continued. The pitch increased in argument.

Another gust of wind nearly blew her slight frame over, and this time caused the coat rack to wobble precariously. It rocked side to side, heavy with its garments. Eliza gasped and rushed to steady it; the floor creaked even louder underfoot. She wondered where her guardian angel voice was as she steadied the coat stand. The fabrics smelled musty and cigar-laden, like an old man.

Eliza picked up a cloak that had fallen, and as she hung it back up, she noticed there were a number of wall hooks hidden behind the coat rack. A neatly labelled collection of keys of various sizes and shapes. There, in the middle, under a brass plate engraved with the word hedge, was a large key with a rounded handle. In her mind, she thanked the absent voice whom she had doubted too quickly. She reached for the key, unbelieving of her luck, but the door handle squeaked. Mr Blythe's displeased voice curled through the crack of the door. Someone was definitely in trouble, and shortly it would be her as well.

Her hand froze just beneath the key as she watched the door edge a little wider. Eliza glanced to the window again, but it seemed too far. Her eyes slid back to the door; she couldn't breathe; she was too frozen to grasp the key. The light of the hall glanced inside when the door opened another inch; it beamed across the floor and drew her attention to a broom leaning in the corner to the left of the window. She lunged for it as the door swung fully open.

Mr Blythe stopped mid-sentence, scolding the Lord's Valet for some kind of misstep when he saw Eliza sweeping the floor.

He cleared his throat. "What are you doing in here, girl?" His eyes fell upon the broom as Eliza swept a little more convincingly. He wandered over to the window, his bushy brows narrowed as he pulled it closed. "Hmm," He rubbed under his nose with a fat finger. "Out with you, I've work to attend."

FOUR

The sisters awaited Eliza behind a Grecian statue the Lord had gifted the Lady upon her last birthday. It had been all the household could talk about when it arrived. It was scandalously naked in all the places that made Eliza blush and the sisters giggle. Sybilla poked a stick at the part hidden behind a hastily added fig leaf. Lady Norlane had been unable to look at the statue without feeling faint, so the Lord had a local mason add modesty to it. Annabelle was trying to peer up underneath it.

Margaret screwed her mouth into a twist as Eliza arrived. "You're late." She peered beyond Eliza, ensuring they were alone.

Eliza handed Margaret the tartlets. She unwrapped the linen, and Annabelle snatched one and rammed it most un-ladylike into her mouth. Sybilla poked her arm. "You didn't eat your luncheon; spit it out!" Annabelle chewed faster. Sybilla smacked her face. Annabelle's cheeks tinted red; tears welled in her lashes. Her fists clenched until she could no longer hold her sobs inside. She coughed and spat pink mush onto the path.

Margaret smiled and tucked the other tartlets into the pocket of her finely embroidered apron. "Time is of the essence," Margaret waved everyone to follow her along the path. Eliza walked obediently behind them; hands clenched in front of her. The sun warmed her back until the clouds obscured it. Afternoon light dulled, a gentle breeze carried the smell of fresh bread from the open kitchen windows, and it gave small comfort to Eliza until they reached the shade of the hedgerow.

Margaret's hand shot out as they stood before its greyed gate. "The key?" Impatience wriggled her long, perfectly clean fingers.

Sweat drizzled down Eliza's back. She stared at the place that enticed her from her room the previous evening. She rolled her thumb over the prick on her finger. The hedgerow looked no more welcoming in daylight.

Eliza swallowed hard, eyes sweeping from one sister to another. Annabelle was still wiping tears and jam from her face as the breeze rustled the leaves of the hedgerow, demanding her attention. Eliza felt small, like she might fold up and disappear under the immensity of it. Then there were the sisters staring at her, arms crossed. Disappearing would be ideal. She had no key to offer. She was going to get a beating today.

Eliza's mind raced with explanations for her failure, rushed with ideas of how to evade the sisters' wrath. The hedgerow's shadow expanded like a hand reaching down to grasp her, just like the shadows in her room. She took a step back. Something tapped against her thigh, but she ignored the sensation as the shadow seemed to follow her. Fear seized her throat and she stepped back again. The Galdrewold was only feet away. Its mysteries known and unknown, ready to swallow her up. She would be more invisible than ever beyond the hedgerow, more invisible than a servant could ever be. Being a no one allowed the sisters to have their way with her. In this life, Eliza was nothing, a fear-ridden blight that bent to the will of mal-intent out of pure and unbridled fear. Through her panic, a singular voice sang softly once more in her ears, and she reached out for it with her heart as Margaret snarled at her.

"Give me the key, Eliza, or Sybilla will wrench it from your filthy hand!" Margaret lunged. Eliza shied away from her snatching fingers. She felt a tap again against her leg. Eliza slid her hand into her apron pocket; it jerked back immediately. Confusion made her dizzy again. She leaned forward, resting a hand on one hip to get blood back into her head. The gravel path faded in and out; its little cream stones looked close and then far. Deep breaths cleared the haze. Sybilla's grinding voice made her fingers bite into her thighs. Her teeth ground until they squeaked.

"Last chance," Sybilla demanded. She stamped her foot just beyond Eliza's field of vision. The crunch was similar to Mrs Embrey flaying a chicken to roast. Eliza imagined doing it to Sybilla. The enticing voice behind her ear became more excitable, blotting out Sybilla's voice, applauding Eliza's frightful thoughts. The words were a murmur she wanted to hear more of. The soft lull paid heed to her loneliness when no one else did.

"I shall not ask you again," Margaret pushed Eliza's shoulder, forcing her to stumble back. Margaret's mouth was moving, but Eliza did not hear her as she focused on the friend in her mind. She listened to the gentle cadence urging her to explore what was in her pocket. Her fingers worked quickly over the cool object. A strange wave of warmth rushed through her; fear drowned in the embrace of it. The voices' excitement grew as her fingers slid around the smooth metal and grasped it tight. The hedgerow's shadow lengthened to catch her for every step she took backwards. The sun breached the clouds overhead, yet the hedgerow's fingers of darkness kept its warmth from her.

The voice cooed at her to move forwards, to embrace the shadows, to hand the key over. Eliza bit her lips, blinked the confusion from her mind. As nothing made any sense, she defaulted to pondering if this was just another dream or moment of mania. Yet, she felt everything more keenly than ever. The heat beneath her skin, the smell of roses and rot blended together, the creak of the hedgerow and the cool clutch of its shadow around her.

Its leaves wafted gently behind the impatient glares of the sisters. They seemed to blur as they moved. The day was clear, the breeze soft, yet the leaves lapped briskly against each other. Eliza bit her bottom lip harder; she tasted blood. She had to be awake.

A tiny pale flower, identical to the previous night, burst open just to the right of the gate. Its blossom purest white, its centre blood red. Eliza stared at it, realising that perhaps last night was more real than she cared to admit. The bloom moved; it turned slowly, its petals closing into a point until it was left facing towards the lock of the old gate. The whispers increased in intensity.

"What is she doing?" Sybilla grumbled as Eliza moved past them and reached for the strange bloom. As her finger touched it, the petals greyed and wilted to dust.

Caught in the intoxicating moment, Eliza did not notice Sybilla move. She yanked Eliza's hair, jerking her back to reality, silencing the murmur that had dulled the slither of the fear in her veins. Eliza wobbled backwards but managed to avoid falling. She blinked hard to contain a rush of tears, kept tremoring hands busy as she thrust them back into her pockets, her right hand tight around the key. Sybilla lunged again and pulled Eliza's arms until they were forced out of the pockets. She wrenched the key out of her fingers and shoved Eliza to the ground.

"She was hiding it!" Sybilla snapped, waving the key in Eliza's face.

Eliza pulled her knees up, her hands shielded her head, awaiting another strike. All she felt was the pound of her own pulse. The sisters began fighting over the key. Eliza pulled her cap back on, pressed her lips tight to suppress the quiver of her chin. She rose to her feet, lifted by the voice. Her chest felt heavy; she clenched her hands into balls. Her cheeks prickled with heat; her skin felt too tight, as though she might burst inside out.

Margaret snatched the key from Sybilla, "Give it here," she held it up too high for the others to reach and turned for the gate. She stopped and peered over her shoulder towards Eliza. Margaret shook her head and held a hand over her heart. "Oh my, how remiss of me. I did forget that cap I promised you, didn't I?" She made a sad face. "So sorry, I just couldn't find one that would at all suit such a… a… an ordinary head. You seem to have found a little something more to your position that suits you quite well anyway." She laughed. "Looks like your reward for your services will be the honour of being in our presence," She sneered and turned back towards the hedgerow.

Whilst the sisters jostled excitedly at the old gate, Eliza's nails raked at her wrists. She stared at them and thought of the kitchen knife. She shook her head, frightened by the thoughts. The voice elevated, scolded her for suppressing her desires. Eliza's legs became restless; she wanted to run and scream, to beat the life out of the sisters. The voice cheered; its encouraging vibrations joined by an orchestral choir of others. So much noise, Eliza pressed her hands against her ears, but the companions of her mind remained.

Fear rose again for a very different reason. These thoughts of hurting people and wishing them ill, they terrified and excited her. Perhaps her guardian was the Devil. Her heart thumped hard. Eliza hugged her belly, squeezed her eyes shut and pushed her thoughts elsewhere. Away from the sisters, afar from the steaming laundry and sweet smells of Mrs Embrey's kitchen. Beyond the stinking chamber pots and endless floor scrubbing. She smudged memories of Lord Norlane's reflection leering at her as she polished the silverware, of the squeak of her door at night, of the pressure of him upon her. She gulped and squeezed her eyes tighter, then took a step forwards, just as the loudest of the voices told her to. Eliza's eyes snapped open to the sound of the sisters still screeching at each other.

"You do it then!" Sybilla muttered through her teeth. She kicked at the still-locked gate, it rattled on ancient hinges. Sybilla elbowed Margaret in her ribcage. Margaret slapped Sybilla's face and snatched the key back. "Move!" Margaret grunted. Sybilla backed away, her eyes thin, her mouth an angry pucker. All the while, Annabelle twirled a ribbon back and forth through her fingers as she plaited it around a doll's neck, delight in her eyes now she'd recovered from the tartlet incident.

Margaret slid the key into the rusted lock, glanced at Sybilla, huffed at her with a smug expression, and twisted to the right. The key did not move. Sybilla laughed.

Margaret glared at Sybilla. "Shut up, you silly cow!" Margaret shook her head and took a calming breath. "It can't be that difficult," She jiggled the key and turned again. It merely squeaked in the immovable lock. Margaret peered over at them all, her back stiffened, and she cleared her throat. Another twist. The gate rattled, the leaves rustled, the key remained immobile. Margaret hit the gate with her free hand, pulled the key out, covered it in her palms and discreetly spat on it. She reinserted it, this time jostling the lock more forcefully. Her arm shook as the key refused to budge.

A giggle rumbled in Eliza's chest, but self-preservation taught her better, so she suppressed it and quietly enjoyed watching Margaret push and pull until her cheeks were pink. Margaret wrestled the lock until wood splintered around the keyhole. She kicked the gate. "Stupid thing!" Margaret snatched a handful of leaves in temper and ripped them from their branches. A malodorous gust burst from within the hedgerow. It caught the leaves from her grasp, twirled them upwards into a vortex over the sisters. Annabelle screeched and fell back onto the lawn. "It's a ghost!"

Sybilla groaned. "Stop being a baby, it's just a gust of wind, you stupid girl." The breeze sighed, and the leaves fluttered over the hedgerow and away into the beyond. "See," Sybilla grumbled. Annabelle's pallor blossomed into an inquisitive bloom again. "Silly me," she stammered but kept her doll close to her chest and stayed well behind Sybilla.

The greenery about the doorway quivered and crackled, the shadows around them deepened. Margaret recoiled, "Must be vermin in it." Her face wrinkled. Her shoes scored the gravel as she shuffled back, hands-on-hips peering up and down the hedgerow's length. Margaret fiddled with her own crucifix as the stirring within the hedgerow settled.

"Me, me! I'll do it! I don't care if I see a rat! I'll catch it and hang it by its scrawny neck!" Annabelle jumped up and down, the doll dangled from its noose. She rustled her hands in the leaves as though to prove her bravery. Margaret pulled her back, Annabelle's doll caught on a branch and hung limply amongst the leaves.

"Don't be ridiculous, Annabelle! If I can't open it, how at all do you suppose you can?" Margaret shoved

Annabelle back behind her, plucked the doll out and threw it at Annabelle's feet. The delicate face cracked.

Eliza felt unexpected delight watching the sisters scuffle amongst each other, bickering like chickens over scraps. All the while, the gate to the Galdrewold remained firmly sealed. Then, the leaves began to flicker once more and the voices harmonised like angels to Eliza. She breathed deeply at their gentle song.

As the sun dipped behind a larger billowing mass of clouds, Eliza watched on quietly as the sisters fought still. Thunder rumbled far in the distance; a spittle of rain eased the fire of Eliza's cheeks. A soft wind toyed with the hem of her dress. The air smelled of lichen and rain, the thunder deepened, and the sound of the sisters squalling raked through Eliza like nails on a board.

It took for Sybilla to push Margaret to the ground before any of them noticed Eliza's hand reaching out in offer. Margaret rolled onto her knees and stood up, slapping down the creases in her dress. She glanced quickly at the darkening sky; her cheeks quivered. "You utter cow, Sybilla!" Annabelle hid behind Margaret; a smile puffed up her cherubic cheeks, and she pulled the noose tighter on the poor doll. The crack in its face widened.

Sybilla smirked and ignored Margaret, instead, she focused on Eliza's hand and laughed. "You? How do you possibly think those twiggy arms are going to open the damned gate?" Thunder rumbled softly again. Sybilla cocked her head towards the sky and sniffed, her mouth thin with annoyance.

Eliza kept her hand open, waiting for the key. Calm draped over her as she focused on the sounds beyond the divide. Chirps, flutters and shuffles in undergrowth and whispers of things unknown. Another splash of light rain ran down her collar.

"Give it to her!" Annabelle jumped up and down, her high-pitched squeal assaulted the momentary peace in Eliza's mind.

"I want to see her snap her arm!" Annabelle giggled. Eliza's eyes slid towards Annabelle. The breeze strengthened, and the last of the sun's warmth slipped behind the hedgerow's shadow. Bird song on this side of the divide stilled, yet the sounds beyond intensified. Eliza's hand remained where it was, waiting for the key.

Annabelle's delight waned, and she slid back behind Margaret. Eyes a little wider, her blush of morbid excitement paled, Annabelle pushed Margaret's hand towards Eliza. "Give it to her, Margy," Annabelle's voice wavered as she clutched onto the back of Margaret's dress.

"Ugh! Fine." Margaret slapped the key into Eliza's palm as hard as she could. Thunder clapped overhead. A light drizzle settled in. Margaret hugged herself, Annabelle snuggled closer into her, Sybilla crossed her arms and snapped at Eliza. "Hurry up!"

Eliza rolled the cool metal in her palm. Its weight was satisfying. She stepped up to the gate; its whorls and cracks reflected the way her insides felt. Her hand pressed gently against its ancient texture. Warmth fanned throughout her chest. The sky darkened further; raindrops slid down her arm as her fingers dipped into its splintery imperfections. Thunder cracked like a whip overhead. Annabelle whimpered. "I don't like thunder." Sybilla shushed her.

Eliza brought the key to the lock. It slid in with ease. She closed her eyes as the whispers grew more excitable. The groan of the hedgerow snapped in time with the wind. The key turned.

Eliza pushed the gate. It creaked open a foot or so before she was muscled aside by the sisters who rushed through ahead of her. Sybilla turned momentarily to glare at her with the unbridled hatred of being shown up. Then, she spat on the ground and ran off, following the others, spoiling the perfect stillness of the Galdrewold.

FIVE

Eliza hesitated at the entrance to the forest. She watched the sisters tread with cautious excitement into a dense verdigris undergrowth. They held up their dresses from the dirt, their disappearing silhouettes lit only by fingers of overcast daylight. A mist blanketed the ground in the distance. The voice in her head remained a soft coo that calmed a new wave of fear that coiled within her. Eliza breathed deep of the forest's swampy breath and peered back through the gateway. She cringed under the vastness of Norlane Hall, watched a carriage pull up outside its grand entrance. The Lord's belly preceded him as he exited the carriage. Eliza hesitated no longer and stepped through.

Eliza caught up with the sisters after Annabelle had tripped over. Margaret picked her up. "Stop being a baby. It's just a scratch!"

"It hurts Margy," Annabelle sobbed. Her strangled doll now dragged behind her in the muddy undergrowth, only half a face left. Margaret inspected the tear in Annabelle's dress and peered back at Eliza. "Don't worry, she'll darn it this evening." Her perfect hair was sodden, and the sight pleased Eliza.

Margaret pointed at Eliza. "You go on ahead, make sure there's nothing else for us to trip on!" Eliza hesitated, not knowing which direction to take. Sybilla backtracked and pushed Eliza hard in the back. Eliza walked on straight ahead, hesitant, but with no other option.

The wild forest had no path, no obvious way to move, other than back towards the manor behind them. Eliza peered over her shoulder, but the hedgerow was no longer visible. They had only walked a few minutes; could they have gone so far as to already lose sight of civilisation? Frigid air nipped through her damp clothes. Fear poked at her thoughts, but the whispers quickly dulled the ache, and she let her balled fists relax by her sides. She took a few more steps forward and breathed in the earthy air. Spirals of frost twisted around her feet. It coiled left and then twirled right as though it had a mind of its own. She was not sure which way to go but spied the mossy remains of an ancient well and stopped next to it. The miasma was denser to the right of the well, she turned that way, and the voices became louder. Eliza heeded them and followed the misty pathway, the sisters whispering excitedly behind her.

With each step, light lost its fight against the canopy overhead, but its cover, at least, filtered the rain. The howl of the brewing storm raged beyond its protection, and Eliza hurried along. As the sisters fussed and squabbled, Eliza concentrated on the murmurs of encouragement that faded when she took a wrong turn and deepened when her path seemed right.

She jumped a ditch and pushed through a dense, slippery fernery until she came to the edge of the fog. It stopped as though there was an invisible barrier holding it at bay. The mist swirled up and back over itself, covering the lower half of her body, deepening the chill. The weather seeped down through cracks in the canopy, bringing with it larger drops of rain.

Things scattered in the leaf litter where her sodden boots sunk. An aching cold wicked through to her stockings. She stood at the edge of the fog, wondering which way to go on.

Seeing her hesitation, Sybilla snapped. "Just keep going straight." Eliza received another shove and fell back into step as Sybilla chatted in hushed tones with the others.

"They say the middle of the forest is haunted. An island surrounded by a small stream. Let's go there." Sybilla shoved Eliza again. "Hurry up."

The wind picked up a notch the deeper they ventured. It felt like a warning generated by the forest itself. Ancient sentinels laced with vines groaned under its gusts. Eliza tightened her cap as her hair fluttered across her face. She hugged herself against the cold and uncertainty. Her boots waded through a sea of umber slipperiness. There was only the occasional tweet of a bird now fleeing the cracks of thunder and lightning that sliced through the canopy. She shivered.

"How will we know when we find it?" Annabelle asked, clinging again to Margaret's dress.

"It will be on an island!" Sybilla yelled over the howl. "You're such an imbecile!"

"I hope it's haunted; I want to see Eliza scream," Margaret's laugh lacked conviction.

"I don't want to see ghosts!" Annabelle squealed. She clutched her doll tighter against her chest.

"Really? Happy to put a noose around anything that moves but scared of a ghost?" Sybilla pulled Annabelle along, but not before snatching her doll from her and throwing it away. "Stop being ridiculous, you're fourteen, that's far too old for dolls anyway!"

Annabelle began to sob, so much so that Margaret gave her another tartlet to quiet her.

Eliza continued on, thinking a ghost perhaps would be less frightening than the sisters. Annabelle grumbled to her right, complaining of the cold. It bit like ice. Eliza shoved her hands deep into her pockets, but they offered no comfort. The dark surroundings held a heavier, heady note of swampy rot. Her feet were now numb.

"Can you hear that?" Margaret stopped, pulled Sybilla to a halt and cocked her ear up. The sound of water trickling only just overcame the grumbling weather. "Sounds close. That way," Sybilla pointed ahead, but Eliza was already moving in that direction. Something whipped her heart with a touch of excitement. A branch creaked overhead. The sisters squealed, then giggled as a crow settled upon it before fluttering quickly away along the path of the wind. Eliza kept a brisk pace; the voices urged her to hurry.

She pushed through a drapery of willow to happen upon the edge of a shallow river bed. It bubbled wildly; its coffers filled upstream by the wild rain beyond. Across the other side, a new fog laced the water's edge. Its white veil petered away near the base of a mounded clearing shadowed by the canopy of a large yew tree. So ancient was it that its uppermost branches were engulfed within the forest's murky night.

"This must be it!" Margaret exclaimed; the clap of her hands echoed through the dense surroundings. She ran on ahead with her sisters towards a small bridge that joined the island to the rest of the forest. They jostled at the bridge, pushing each other to cross first.

Eliza weaved her fingers together, clasping and unclasping, entranced by the yew. The tree's gnarled branches entwined into leafless knots, filled with shadows, nooks of darkness, places to hide and never be found. The ground below erupted with thick moss-covered roots feeding the goliath.

The air felt colder than before, yet Eliza wiped a spring of sweat from her palms. The cold nipped at her ears; mist curled around her hips. She stepped away from its cool grasp, but it seemed to follow her. Whispers chorused the loudest voice. The sounds of the sisters dulled. With each melodic beat in her head, Eliza moved towards the bridge, drawn by the voices. Knee-high ferns, wet with dew, added to the damp of her dress. She shivered once more as she came to a stop. The sisters bickered in the middle of the bridge.

Sybilla jumped up and down, her shoes clipped on the ancient planks. "You'll fall in!" She wobbled the balustrade. The wind blew in strong gusts along the burgeoning stream. It pulled her hair wild, toppled Annabelle into Margaret. Annabelle screamed as they caught themselves from slipping over. Margaret slapped her hand over Annabelle's mouth and pointed at Sybilla. "Stop it, Sybilla! Do you want us to get caught out here?" Margaret steadied herself against the balustrade. "It will be you that takes the punishment."

Margaret glared down at Annabelle. "Are you going to scream again?" Annabelle shook her head. "Good, if you do, I'll tell the vicar what you do to your dolls," Margaret grimaced. "How many Hail Mary's will that be?" Annabelle screwed up her face when Margaret let her go and crossed her arms. Margaret peered over her shoulder. "Hurry up, Eliza, are *you* scared?" The three of them laughed. "Come, you can find some ghosts with us. Probably will be the most exciting thing you've done in your miserable little life," Margaret's brows tweaked, her mouth pulled into a half-smile.

Eliza's jaw ached, lips pressed firm, she held her tongue as always. She stepped a little closer, eyes wide. The trees whispered, leaves trilled high and low. Boughs creaked; twigs snapped. The murky surroundings felt alive with more than furry and feathered things. Her feet sunk deeper in the thickening mud with every step closer to the bridge. She pulled one boot out and took a step closer. The voices chittered more excitedly. She peeked quickly over her shoulder, convinced something just had to be behind her — nothing but the greens and browns of the forest and the roiling fog that trailed her.

Eliza wriggled her freezing fingers; her little finger found another loose thread in her pocket. It twirled nervously until the thread tightened and snapped. She pressed her lips together, wished she was in the laundry surrounded by steam with Agnes curled up nearby. Instead, she rested a hand upon the splintered railing. Her eyes ran up the length of the yew tree at the centre of the island.

She stepped onto the bridge; dampness squelched between her toes. The sisters jostled each other to step onto the island first as thunder rumbled louder, lightning flashed through cracks in the leafy ceiling. Eliza felt its power rattle the bridge; her fingers gripped tight to the railing. She stared at the tree. Something moved within it; her grip tightened further. A flicker that was there and then not there. Margaret grabbed her arm, and Eliza nearly jumped out of her skin.

"Go on, you first," she pushed Eliza ahead of them. Her boots sunk into a dark and powdery ground, untouched by the rain. The wind swirled faster on this side of the river, whipped her dress up and tugged at her cap. It smelled of old things, burnt things, dead things.

Eliza shielded her face from swirling debris. Her squinted eyes took in as much of the scenery as they could before the sisters took control. Her body shivered harder and she moved purely to generate warmth. Wandering cautiously across a grassless expanse, she sat upon one of three undulating rocks below the tree. The rock underneath her was soft with moss, a small comfort in a miserable situation. Eliza hugged herself against the weather. The girls bustled across and wandered about the yew, poking its bark, climbing its great roots. Annabelle stomped on a clutch of mushrooms at its base. The wind gusted harder.

Eliza stayed where she was, observing the tree. Its bark was unusual, cracked and peeled back in places. One of the roots was split wide, its inner flesh grey, as though it was dead. As the thought slipped through her mind, a shudder rumbled beneath her feet, a drumming reverberation followed. Eliza jumped up, looked down upon the furry rock. The ground pulsed beneath her feet again; the voices trilled. She leaned forwards and sunk her hands into the green velvet covering; it too pulsed with the same beat. She felt like she could sink within it.

The sisters ran past Eliza, pulling her from the strange reverie. Annabelle yanked at Eliza's dress and then ran back to the yew and climbed over its roots some more. They picked at its trunk, peeled its skin away. The voices hissed, and a welcome heat flushed Eliza's cheeks.

Sybilla jumped upon another root, hands-on-hips. "Look at this place! Ugh! I wouldn't imagine even a ghost would see fit to live here." Sybilla jumped back down, scooped up a handful of soil and drizzled the charcoal-like earth from her hand. She wobbled in the gusts that threaded through the forest. Her hair blew wildly; a ribbon slipped from it and disappeared upon mother nature's wrath.

"It's the ugliest thing I've ever seen!" Margaret steadied herself against the trunk.

"I don't like it!" Annabelle said as she poked moss from another rock with a stick.

I love it, Eliza thought to herself. She liked the swampy taste of the air, the softness underfoot, the pull of the whispers that were louder and more joyful than ever.

"Look! Up there!" Annabelle was suddenly wrought with thrill again. "Decorations. I want one. I want one now!"

Intrigued, Eliza set around the offside of the yew. Tucked in the shadows and niches of the boughs, a myriad of unusual wooden decorations hung still and untouched by the wind. Made of twigs and leaves, some with feathers and leaves entwined. Some were circular, some square, and more than a few were in the shape of a star within a circle. A handful were in the design of human torsos.

Eliza stepped away and sat back upon the closest velveteen rock. She focused on the dark recesses and studied the symbols with interest. The heartbeat beneath her intensified as she counted three human effigies, three circles with stars inside and two squares strung like a harp and woven with feathers.

Margaret shouted quite suddenly. "They're hexes!" The ground thrummed harder. Eliza shifted on the rock, but the pulsing kept in tune with her own heartbeat. She did not understand how the sisters had not commented on it.

The girls skipped about the base of the yew, jumping up and down, grasping for hangings. Heavier rain penetrated the canopy in thick, freezing droplets. The Galdrewold shaded to the dark of night in the middle of the day. The sisters squealed, danced hand in hand, soaked.

"What are you doing just sitting there? Come dance with us, Eliza." Margaret yelled over the squalling weather. She picked up a large stick to poke at a feather-woven star.

Eliza's fingers curled into fists, affronted by the disrespect. Her hands stung. She stared at the half-moon crescents her nails had left behind. Blood settled in the creases of her palms. It darkened quickly, becoming thick and sticky. She imagined it was the blood of the sisters, and she dug into her palms again until blood oozed through the cracks of her fingers. She opened her hands, let the blood drip away. The mist recoiled; the char of the ground drank each plum drop. The fog swirled back into place, its blanket rich with shadows and movement.

Eliza reached into her mind, searched for the strongest of the voices. Anger seared within her in a most disproportionate manner. As she shook with emotions that made no sense, the loudest voice sung above the others. Calm flowed into her limbs, and a comforting, gentle warmth tempered her rage as she watched the sisters desecrate the yew.

"This is a witch's tree!" Sybilla's screech jolted Eliza's attention from the shadows in the fog. Sybilla walked the circumference, arms crossed. "I've heard the rumours, the whispers of the adults about keeping children away from the forest." She stopped and put her hands on her hips, just below the pale satin ribbon Lady Norlane forced her to wear about her waist. "They say, the ones that look like people are those that the tree has…." Sybilla stopped in her tracks.

Eliza's hands bunched her apron, her dry mouth wetted. Her skin tingled; a smile urged at her mouth as she watched Sybilla. Margaret and Annabelle stopped mid-dance, their arms limp at their sides. "What, Sybilla? They say what?" Margaret demanded.

Sybilla's fingers began to twitch, her head ticked to the right, and a growl rumbled from her. Eliza leaned backwards; she covered the widening smile with her hand. A strange excitement welled within her, it oozed through her belly and urged her heart into a faster pace.

The wind howled. The yew remained still and silent.

"Margy, what's wrong with her?" Annabelle whimpered.

Sybilla turned around in slow, jittery jerks. Her mouth agape, her eyes wide. She lunged for her sisters and screamed. Margaret hit the ground, tripped up by Annabelle. Sybilla bent over in a coughing fit of laughter, so much so, she too fell to the ground. All three slick with ashy mud, they pushed themselves back to their feet.

"You evil witch of a sister!" Margaret yelled, slapping down her filthy dress. Margaret flicked a clump of mud from her arm, then swung her hand across Sybilla's cheek. Sybilla pressed against the welt, her eyes thin. "Clearly, you can only jest at others, *Margy!*" Sybilla glanced at Eliza.

Annabelle slithered in next to Margaret, her mouth screwed up. "If you were a doll, you would be dead, Sybilla!" Annabelle sniffed. Margaret put a finger to her lips to hush Annabelle.

"That was *not* funny," Margaret snapped. "You do realise we are going to have to hide these clothes from Mother now, lest you want a beating or worse, miss the Henley's party," Margaret mumbled to herself as she brushed away more mud.

The sight of them covered in mud, less than perfect and proper, sent a darker thrill through Eliza. Where the light of prayer left her empty, something heavy wormed its way inside her. Their discomfort filled her with syrupy pleasure, and she welcomed it.

Margaret huffed loudly, pinched her cheeks, her voice once more measured. "Now, Sybilla, that means we will have to sneak our garments to the laundry. Your behaviour causes us to venture to the cesspit where that thing lives and works." Margaret pointed back at Eliza without looking at her. Margaret tucked her slick hair in place as best as she could and knotted a ribbon at the nape of her neck. She did the same for Annabelle and slipped back on her petite shoe that had become wedged into the sticky ground.

Sybilla rubbed at the handprint on her cheek. "You two are pathetic. It was a lark, that's all!" The fingerprints disappeared under a new flush of excitement. Sybilla's eyes widened as she tapped her temple. "Just imagine the fun we can have." She pointed up to the tree. "Imagine leaving one of these at church!" She laughed and slapped her thick fingers against the trunk. "Under the alter, no, on the front door for all to see on Sunday!"

A branch cracked and dropped from above. Sybilla dove away, face-first into the slosh of the ground. It was the others turn to laugh as Sybilla peeled a fat, wet leaf from her face. "Disgusting!" Sybilla spat a clot of mud from her lips, wiped her mouth on the back of her hand. She rubbed her arms briskly to warm against the weather.

"Brrr. It feels like it's going to snow." Annabelle hugged into Margaret.

"Don't be ridiculous, it's just a Spring storm," Margaret responded. Eliza realised she felt as warm as toast; she wondered if she was coming down with a fever. It could explain the murmurings in her head.

Margaret waved her sisters closer. "Look, there are more hexes," She looked back to Eliza. "Come over here," Eliza rose unwillingly, moving to the right of the yew with them. Margaret split the last tartlet into three pieces and handed them to Sybilla and Annabelle. "Sorry," Margaret smiled unapologetically towards Eliza as she ate her piece. Eliza's stomach rumbled. The sisters chewed in brief silence, all looking up into the tree. Eliza stared at her feet, held her stomach, clawed at the nauseating rage.

The storm set in harder. The rain thickened. It hissed through the Galdrewold, harmonised with the wind and thunder. The sisters' dresses fluttered wildly. Annabelle lost another ribbon to the gusts. This one whisked away upon the wind, up into the tree. It snagged in its twists and curls right next to a human effigy.

"My favourite ribbon!" Annabelle cried. "I want to go home; I don't like it here anymore." Her cheeks and nose were rose-red with cold. She tugged at Margaret, who was doing her best to hold her dress down. Sybilla glared up into the tree, pointing. "Look at that. Those hexes aren't even moving," she said.

Margaret backed away. "I think…" she gulped and glanced over her shoulder not once, but twice, to the murky depths of the surrounding forest. "I think we should leave. I've…" She cleared her throat and stood taller. "I've had quite enough of this vastly uninteresting place." Both she and Annabelle edged back towards Eliza, and she had a strange urge to push them both towards the tree. Instead, Eliza leaned into the gusts, the cool of it eased her feverish skin.

"No!" Sybilla yelled, attention still on the twiggy decorations that hung as if frozen in time. "I want one of those, especially now." Margaret glanced behind her at Eliza.

"You… you go get one so we can get out of here. I'm wet through and want to change."

The whispers stopped with a suddenness that made Eliza feel a vacuous loneliness. She backed away, looking for the rock to lean on. It was gone. She spun around; it was nowhere to be seen. None of the strange rocks were anywhere to be seen.

Her body felt sure to give way, the heat in her face drained to her toes. As her knees threatened to buckle, an invisible push steadied her. She felt something under the enormity of this ancient tree, and she was not convinced that taking something from it was anything but playing with fire.

"Hurry up, Eliza. Get me that hex next to Annabelle's ribbon; you can retrieve that for her as well." Sybilla demanded.

Eliza, still looking for the rocks, shook her head.

"You dare to refuse?" Margaret crossed her arms. Eliza remained unmoved.

"Is that how we are going to play? Well, fine then." Margaret trudged through the mud, nose to nose with Eliza.

"Just you remember, girl, I know what goes on in our home. I know what my father gets up to. I've seen him slip downstairs to the servants' quarters. I could easily tell Mother that it is you who secrets into his rooms at night."

Eliza's mouth dropped. Her thumb came back to her wrist, gouging into a scab. Hot liquid slipped into her palm.

"Oh yes, Eliza, I can ruin your life with a single conversation. Mother believes everything I say." Her voice was a high-pitched nervous trill, her face quivered with the fervour of the threat.

"I'll tell everyone you dragged us out here and wished hateful sorcery upon us. Then you will be hanging from the tree just like those repulsive things." She pointed to the hexes, her hand shook. A red blotchiness crept up Margaret's neck and onto her cheeks. "Climb the tree, Eliza, and get all three of us one of those things."

Margaret dragged Eliza by her sleeve towards the yew to a place on the trunk gnarled with cankerous spines. "This looks a good foot up." Margaret pushed Eliza right up to the trunk. Bewitched tree or not, this was not one that invited a person to climb.

"Hurry up, or I'll make you," Sybilla picked up a stick as thick as Eliza's arms. Eliza shook her head again, partly to refuse, partly to shake away the voices excitedly urging her forward.

Sybilla lunged. The wind gusted harder, a wilder howl to its song. Sybilla lost her balance; the branch glanced off Eliza's knee instead of her head. The sting was tolerable, Sybilla's fist that quickly followed through into her stomach, not so. Eliza bent over, coughing through the deep ache in her belly. Her nostrils were tight as she sucked hard for air, to quell the pain, to subdue the need to lunge back.

Eliza raised her head just as Sybilla yelled through her teeth. "Get me one of those hexes, or you will regret this more than you can imagine."

Eliza clutched her middle and sank to her knees. At any moment, her belly could expel its contents, and she swallowed back the burn that threatened more humiliation. Her thoughts were a chaotic mess.

She curled her fingers through the mud; it was cold on the surface, strangely tepid underneath. She clawed in until her fingers could push no further. She felt anchored to something and wished to be swallowed up by it, warm and safe. But the wind blew ever harder, and the rain slapped her senses back.

Eliza peered up the length of the tree as she pushed herself to her feet. She grabbed the trunk for support. For a split second, her vision blackened; she smelled smoke, heard agonised screams. Eliza leaned her head against the yew until the hysteria passed. She rubbed her right ear, wishing it away. She felt sure now that she was entirely insane. The voices did not abate, solidifying her theory of madness. They niggled away, relentlessly, incoherently.

"It's getting colder Eliza, hurry up!" Margaret yelled. Eliza could feel the sisters close behind. She could not run, she could not fight, she had to comply, so she placed one hand on the trunk, in between the shards of bark.

Eliza moved unwillingly, pushed by the return of fear, urged by delirium. She felt sure she may choke on her own heart, yet a glance over her shoulder told her that her only retreat was now cut off by the sisters who blocked the small bridge, eyes wide with excited terror.

Thunder cracked overhead. If it was any darker, it would be night. The wind smelled more rancid, of fire and rot as she got her first foothold and looked up. A bolt of lightning pierced through the canopy; a shadow dashed amongst the branches. Eliza hoped it was a squirrel. She held on tight, hugged the trunk, looked up again as another flash lit the recesses. A moss-covered face peered down at her. Obsidian eyes glistened at her for a fraction of a second, and in the next flash, it was gone. Her breaths were heavy, short, sharp gasps. She could not move. Terror was above and below her.

"Faster, Eliza!" Margaret yelled.

She could not slow her breathing, she was sure to collapse, yet she felt a warmth press upon her, urging her up a notch higher. As another rumble roared overhead, Eliza peered hesitantly up to see shadowy arms reach down to her.

The sisters or the tree? Fear tremored through her fingers, and she dug them in harder to keep her grip. Was it the sisters' threats or the force she felt guiding her? She repeated the question over and over, not noticing her feet had moved until her hand touched the crook of the bough.

"Hurry up!" Margaret yelled again through gritted teeth. "We are going to freeze to death!"

I wish you would, Eliza thought, unable to look down to the ground without feeling giddy. Fog snaked up the tree; the wind edged her torso against the rough bark. The shadowy hands guided her along the length of the bough where the hexes hung. Eliza held on against the storm's wrath. She gritted her teeth and slid an inch at a time. The tree creaked, the air howled, the rain seemed to sink beneath her skin and flood her soul.

The bark was slippery; the thunder made her cower with each cracking rumble. Her arms and legs encircled the branch so tight they began to cramp. The sisters continued to scream their impatience below, yet the voices at least had quelled so she could concentrate. Eliza pulled herself forward, following the course of the shadow hand. It drew her toward a human effigy; she reached for it but slid and grasped the bough, hooked one boot back over it and steadied herself.

"I want the star." Annabelle screeched far below, yet the shadow hand caressed the effigy, urging Eliza towards it. The fog curled around it, immobile and unaffected by the storm. "Eliza, we will leave you here if you don't hurry up this instant!" Margaret yelled, and the sisters began retreating, windswept back across the bridge.

If panic was not already the commander of Eliza, it surged forwards like a dictator. It competed with the shadow, took control and made her clutch frantically for a star hex just a little further out. She slid along painstakingly slow past the effigy. She ignored the shadow that urged her to it. The bough thinned; her grip more perilous. The voices returned, screaming in her mind, angry as she rushed for what Annabelle wanted.

There was another crack, but it was not thunder. The bough lurched. Eliza screeched. Her bloodied nail beds dug under the bark as the branch cracked again under her weight. She reached for the star-shaped symbol, just an inch or two from her fingertips.

"Grab it now!" Sybilla shouted. Eliza gripped the tree for dear life as the bough wobbled up and down.

She was closer to the effigy, but she knew that would not do. Eliza readjusted her legs and scooted another inch as the rain pelted harder. Panting through her nose, she blotted out the voices. They were not of any use as she clung for her life. She was utterly terrified.

With the sisters screeching at her and blinded by the driving rain, Eliza reached again for the star. It was blurry; she blinked the rain away, or tears, or both. Lightning flashed and struck near the tree. Eliza heard a snap. The sisters screamed; the branch shook and shuddered. Eliza gasped; her body clenched. She clung desperately, but her weight swivelled her around and she slid underneath the branch. Legs crossed over the branch, fingers slipping; she gulped heavily for breath. Every muscle was on fire. The blur of the hex was right above her head; she made a last grasp for it. Eliza no longer heard the sisters, she did not feel the rain, the wind was a memory. All she remembered was weightlessness until the bough crushed her against the ground.

SIX

"For the love of Jesus Christ himself!"

Hands pressed against Eliza's forehead; fingers touched the pulse in her neck. Something warm draped over her freezing body.

"Eliza? Can you hear me, child?" Mrs Embrey sounded breathless.

"Least she's breathin'," It seemed to be the gardener's voice. Eliza could smell fresh grass and manure mingled with sweat.

"Those blasted girls, they'll be the death of her," Mrs Embrey's voice quivered with anger. Eliza moaned as someone lifted her from the ground. Her body was moving, but to where she did not know.

"Surprised she's alive, Mrs E. Took all me might to get that there branch off of her," the gardener said.

Eliza groaned. Her chest hurt; everything hurt. "There, there. Let's get you back home and to bed now." Mrs Embrey cooed. Eliza managed to open one eye a slit. Everything was dark, the forest quiet but for the odd chirp and rhythmic crunch of footsteps. Both eyes flickered. She squinted up to the person carrying her. The mossy black-eyed face stared back. Eliza slipped backwards into oblivion.

†

The last thread of faith dissipated in her dreams that night. It dissolved as her injuries drew her from the comfort of sleep. Eliza quite plainly awoke with no belief in God. As her eyes peeled open to a room of shadow and firelight, the voices enveloped her, the loudest whispered deep in her mind. *The flame has been lit.* A rapturous heat slid down her body and blossomed into bliss. A smile pinched the bruises on her face.

An owl squawked as she slid her toes to the floor. Both legs cross-hatched with scrapes, her left arm and head were bandaged. Despite this, the heaviness in her joints was tolerable, and she stood up and stretched. Moonlight struck across her room until halted by the shadows that were a denser black in the corners, creeping out along the walls. She squinted, sure again, something moved to the right of the door, but then the babe cried upstairs; a long colicky howl. Feet lumbered about overhead. Doors opened and closed, but the cries continued.

Eliza looked back to the corner. There was nothing, yet there was something. An unseen presence, a weight upon the air, however, it did not feel malicious. Despite this, her heart thundered against her ribs, and she backed away until her legs hit the edge of her bed. The distinct heavy tang of wet leaves, the smell of the garden after a spring storm, wafted about her. She sniffed under her arms, but she smelled of Mrs Embrey's lavender soap.

Her fingers curled around the bedpost; she sat and stared hard into the corner. The hearth burned brighter with no addition of coal. Amber hues ate at the shadows, and she saw something; she definitely saw something shiny and black in the corner to the right of her door. It was looking at her. Something reached out from the umber. It sliced through the moonlight that struck the door, along the wall, towards Eliza.

The hearth blew out. Eliza jumped up and ran for the door. She jiggled the lock, her fingers shook, they slipped, and the key fell from the lock. It spun across the room to settle under her bed. The thing was there now; two black orbs shone from behind her bed as though it had melded into the wall. Wet footprints glistened on the floorboards just under the window, which she only now noticed was cracked open a few inches. She wondered again, like the other night, if she should flee through it. As though it existed in her thoughts, the shadow oozed over the bed head, its hand elongated under the cindered remnants of the crucifix and down to the side table where her ragged bible sat.

The bed creaked; its mattress sunk under an invisible weight. Teetering on the edge of the table, Eliza's tattered bible shifted ever so slightly as shadow fingers reached out and toppled it over. It thudded softly to the floor, and the shadow oozed down the length of the table, curled around the bible and spun it around a dozen times before it flung across the room, coming to a stop against Eliza's feet. Her toes curled back from its pages, and she pressed her body against the locked door. Frozen, she watched the book vibrate, the cover flicked open, thin, yellowed pages rustled like a thousand butterflies. They flicked back and forth until the bible lay still; just the corners of the open pages fluttered as though inviting her in. She pressed harder against the door, took a step to the left and jiggled the handle knowing full well it was still locked. A rush of heat fanned Eliza, the bible slid left, stopping again at her feet.

She stared at the book; her fingers peeled away from the door. *Pick it up.* The voice was distinct. She balled her fists. The fire relit itself, and the bible quivered. She pulled her hands back to her chest. Dancing with the Devil was what this must be, not the guardian angel she had been hoping for. Surely an angel would not scare her so? But God was no longer in her heart, and that left a space for only devils, not angels.

The book nudged forward again, its weight making a soft *shhh* sound. Eliza pursed her lips to control her exhalations which were too rapid; her lips and fingers tingled. She unwillingly lowered herself, fingers splayed wide as though reaching for poison. The air was heavy, pressing her closer to the book.

There was a moist crunch, like the sound of Mrs Embrey wringing a chicken's neck. Eliza hesitated as her fingers neared the pages. Something fell from overhead. A splash of liquid hit the delicate pages. The hearth crackled louder and brighter than ever. The urge to obey whatever force surrounded her was victorious as Eliza dipped the tip of her finger into the liquid. She smoothed it between finger and thumb. It was slippery and thick and the colour of the secret bottle of Port that Lady Norlane hid in the base of her armoire. She brought it to her nose, it smelled metallic and thickened quickly upon her skin. It was blood.

Eliza was mesmerised by the crimson stain on her fingertips. It tingled, warmed down through her palm and burned along the length of her arm, finishing with a punch in her chest. She slipped to the floor, fell against the door with a thud, gasping. The rhythmic pulse in her ears receded to something new, an abrasive slithering that scraped overhead. She covered her face, the blood smearing under her right eye. She shook her head but knew she had to look up; she just had to.

The ceiling had splintered into a thousand cracks, small crevices pushed open by the creep of a vine. Green leaves, glossy in the moonlight, spilled from within it. It covered the ceiling in moments, creaking and snapping as it grew over her bed and down along the floor. It curled past her and disappeared into the shadows of the farthest corner. Eliza watched in horrified awe until the vine ceased its movement.

Eliza sat in silence. Apart from the roaring hearth, all was quiet, all was still. Another spot of blood dripped onto her leg. When she looked up again, it was only then that she saw the single white flower dripping blood from its centre. She blinked as another drop dribbled onto her brow, over her eye, and down her cheek. She touched it, and now both her hands were smeared with the strange floral blood.

Through the gap of her fingers, she noticed the bible once more, with the dried spot of blood on its page. She reached for the book. Despite overwhelming fear, she was driven by a fantastical thrill, a strange feeling of danger that she was willing to court. Eliza rose up and made her way to her bed where she sat, the bible in her hands, her mind aflutter. Her fingers ran the edges of the book, trailed the neat script, and stopped upon the spot that was stained red. She scanned the words next to it.

1 Samuel 22:23

"Stay with me; don't be afraid. The man who wants to kill you is trying to kill me too. You will be safe with me." Eliza's fingers tapped under the words. *Stay with me; don't be afraid.* She repeated these words in her mind. She wanted to speak out loud, but it had been so long since she allowed herself to speak so as to be heard. She did not know how to begin to pass words through her lips, so she thought her question. *Are you here to help me?*

A warmth wrapped around her, and the fire whooshed. An image of the yew tree flashed into her mind. It was surrounded by those strange white flowers blooming in clusters around the great tree trunk. Women in peasant attire kneeled at its base, picking them, placing some in a basket and some in each other's hair. They laughed. They seemed happy. A young ebony-haired woman turned, looked directly at Eliza as though she was in this vision. She handed Eliza a flower. The vision ended abruptly as the sound of a key scraped into the lock of her door. Eliza dropped the bible and scuttled to the head of her bed.

"Ah, waiting up for me, I see?" Lord Norlane drawled as he stepped in, candle in hand. He did not notice the vine, his eyes only on her and the bed. Eliza felt like she was about to vomit.

Help me! she screamed in her mind, but no voice answered her, no one sang or wooed her. Her body was sore from the fall. She did not want this vile man on top of her again, adding to the pain. She pulled up her covers, pleaded to the shadows but nothing was there, just her and the vulgar smell of sweat and desperation.

The Lord placed his candle by her bedside and his fingers to his lips.

"Now, now, just a little something for the one who gives you a place to call home."

He pushed her onto the mattress. She gagged on his brandy breath and stiffened her body to inhibit the drunken fumbling of his fingers. He was too big, too strong, so she stared at the ceiling and wished him to be done quickly.

The vine began to move again, creeping out of cracks that were not there when she went to bed. Its branches writhed like snakes, slithering in and out of each other. The Lord did not notice a thing as he grunted and farted on top of her. She retched in disgust.

The shadow reappeared and twisted throughout the leaves. Eliza focused on the fantastical sight, wished for it to save her from the beast. The shadow stretched long and thin until an arm shape formed and pulled at a length of vine amongst the tangle. It guided this branch free. Its thorns scraped across the ceiling.

A tear slid from Eliza's left eye, stinging the fresh scrapes on her skin. The shadow reached down to her. An elongated finger of blackness absorbed the sadness from her skin. Its touch was painless whilst the Lord thumped roughly against her leg, too inebriated to know the difference. The rigidity of Eliza's limbs relented as the shadow retreated. A calmness descended upon her as though she had left her body, and she watched with morbid delight as the shadow arm coiled the branch back like a whip.

In that moment, her guardian was not God or an angel; it was not the Devil either. It was an ancient darkness, fulminant with the power to heal and destroy. It was the voices in her head, the taste of the wind, the call in the night. It was the only thing protecting her. Eliza embraced it as a starving man would grasp a morsel of bread.

The shadow flicked the branch. It silently snapped forwards and whipped across Lord Norlane. He yelped, went rigid and rolled from her onto the floor with a thud. Eliza sat up, quickly pulling her nightdress down to find the Lord cowering on the floor, holding his shoulder, the linen of it bloomed red. His bulging eyes met hers as he scrambled to his feet. He stumbled towards the light in the hallway, tripped on a length of vine and fell against the wall. He moaned incoherently, grasped for the handle and rattled the door to escape. He turned a moment and stared at Eliza, confusion or fear, she was not sure. His face was swollen and bilious, he looked like a pig about to explode. Eliza giggled behind her hands. Lord Norlane glared at her and pointed. "You... you, you're a...." He belched the smell of stale alcohol before he could finish his slurred accusation. He pressed his limp blood-soaked arm up against his chest as he fumbled with the doorknob again. It clicked, he glanced back at Eliza, then stumbled out, the door left open.

Eliza sat in silence for a moment, huddled into her knees. She peered up to the roof, but the vine was no longer there, the cracks repaired, her shadow saviour gone. She reached for the candle Lord Norlane left behind and clicked her door fully closed, her ear against it, listening to him thump away down the corridor.

She made her way to the washstand, somehow lighter on her feet. Eliza leaned into the wood and grit her teeth before pouring a little water into the bowl. She dipped a cloth into it and wiped away all traces of him. Her thumb twitched to dig into her skin. Her fingertips clutched harder into the washstand. She lifted her head and looked at the mirror.

The wound from Lady Norlane had bruised; her eyes were heavy and dark underneath. Her lips dry and cracked, the skin dark and hard, yet she smiled at herself. Warmth blossomed within her; she relaxed and stared into the reflection as she noticed she was not alone at all. The shadow remained, a blurred essence, silently watching on from the far wall.

She nodded in thanks to it, and as though waiting for her invitation, it slid around the walls towards her. A human-shaped visage rose slowly behind her, blurred at its edges, featureless, apart from eyes as black as ink that glistened down at her. The smell of moss and rot was strong. Eliza reached out; her fingertips touched its reflection. The darkness embraced her, sunk beneath her skin and melded with the shell that she was. It gave her a comfort that no light had ever done. She felt it writhe around inside until it slipped around her heart and took control of each frantic beat. The shadow guardian soothed her pain and eased the chaos in her mind. It obliterated fear.

SEVEN

The warmth of dawn sunlight awoke Eliza. A comforting sweetness turned her head to find a breakfast tray on her side table with tea and toast. *Mrs Embrey,* she thought with love. She hungrily eyed a pot of plum preserve. For a moment, she had forgotten the happenings of the night, and when it did enter her thoughts, she passed it off as another dream, yet the memory and comfort of the shadow were strong, and a delicious warmth spread from her belly up through her chest like a hug.

Eliza flung the covers away. Her nightgown was unruffled, her intimate areas free of pain. Eliza drew in a relieved breath, pushed herself up and made her way to the window. Dust motes scattered as she reached through the sun's kiss and rested her hand on the warm glass. A cerulean sky capped the hedgerow. The morning glow seemed to lessen its mystery.

Hunger called, and she reached for the breakfast tray. The tea was hot, the toast thickly buttered, and the preserve sticky and sweet. She took her time, no urge to hurry. As she flicked toast crumbs from her lap, Eliza noticed something sticking out from under the bed. She reached to the floorboards and retrieved the shrivelled remains of a white blossom with a blood-red centre.

Eliza dropped it as though it were a hot coal. Her eyes shot to the ceiling. It was as it should be, just a ceiling in no need of repair. The hearth had dulled to gently glowing embers, her door closed, with the key present and turned to the right. Then she saw the Lord's candle on the floor, its silver holder upside down, and a small scorch mark on the boards. Eliza scuttled back into bed and pulled the quilt up to her chin.

Panic tightened her chest. A lump of half-chewed toast became stuck in her throat. She pounded at her chest until she coughed it out onto the quilt.

The sunlight no longer felt comforting. Eliza darted out of bed before the thought fully formed and snatched up the candlestick. She reached over the hearth; it was still warm but not too hot, ran her fingers along the grooves up inside the chimney and searched for a ledge of brick. It was hotter up there, and her fingers burned as she fumbled about. On the far side, though, she found what she needed, a little out-cropping of the flue. She pushed the evidence of the Lord's visit onto it.

Her door jiggled and swung open; Eliza nearly toppled straight into the embers.

"What on God's good earth are you doing, Eliza?" Mrs Embrey's brows rose then furrowed quickly into the middle. Eliza jumped up, rolling her blackened palms over each other before quickly rinsing them in her basin.

"Hmph! Well, if you've energy enough to play in the cinders, you're certainly in fine shape to get back to work." She waddled over to her and unwound Eliza's bandages. Mrs Embrey stood back and tapped her lips with a stubby finger. "My word Eliza, you've naught anything so much as a scratch left!" She stuffed the bandages into her pocket, shook her head, mumbled something that might have been a prayer. "Wash yourself up now," Mrs Embrey wandered to the window, her feet soft rhythmic slaps on the floor. She opened it up and began to pack up the breakfast tray. Eliza winced as she stood on the white bloom. It hurt somehow. Mrs Embrey turned about, eyes running the length of Eliza and wandered towards her washstand.

"You can go straight…" The baby began to cry upstairs. Mrs Embrey tutted to herself and poured a little fresh water into the basin. "As I was saying, go straight to work in the washroom when you've made yourself more respectable. The family have taken breakfast in their rooms this morning. The…" The babe's scream heightened. Mrs Embrey's shoulders slumped a little, and she performed the sign of the cross. "Upon my word, the Devil has his grasp on this household. What with the Lord taken ill overnight and that poor ignored babe…" Lips pursed, she shook her head. "Hurry up now. I'll go find Nanny or tend the poor lad myself. Stay away from the Lord and Lady's chambers. You're not to disturb them today. Also, you're to leave the sisters chambers for other staff to tend to. They're confined to their rooms as punishment for going into the forest. And…" Mrs Embrey barely suppressed the delighted glint in her eyes. "They are no longer going to the Henley's garden party."

A gush of fresh morning air rushed through the curtains, cool and refreshing. Sunlight haloed around Mrs Embrey. Eliza smiled wider than ever as she gazed past her, thanking the shadow guardian for being real, not a hopeless dream. She closed her eyes and breathed in the forest air. She barely heard her name being called.

"Eliza!" Mrs Embrey's voice snapped with annoyance. "What is wrong with you?"

Eliza opened her eyes, her smile still an unfamiliar feeling pushing at her cheekbones.

Mrs Embrey edged the tray against her soft hip, leaned over and placed the back of her hand against Eliza's forehead. "Are you unwell? You never smile." Her face creased with worry. "Your eyes are glassy," The cook put the tray down and poured the last of the tea. "Here now, fortify yourself and go to the larder to fetch more unguent for your lips. They're awfully dry." Eliza swallowed the dark brew, her attention magnetised towards the hedgerow.

Mrs Embrey's thumb and forefinger ran down Eliza's face to meet at her chin. She tipped Eliza's contented face up to hers. "Have those girls finally sent you mad?" Mrs Embrey's eyes moistened; she swallowed emotion away as she gently rubbed Eliza's chin. "Stay away from them, my dear. You're a good soul. Don't let them corrupt your innocence. I don't know what I'd do without you here." She sniffed, blinked her eyes rapidly and pulled her apron up to her nose to wipe it.

"Well then, hurry yourself up. There's work to be done." Mrs Embrey plucked up the tray, rattling the cup and pot together. "Get on with you then. Make haste. There's a lot of laundry today. I expect it will keep you busy and out of trouble. I've already filled the copper for you."

Eliza washed slowly. She felt no urgency, no rush, no desire to please. She concentrated on her nails that had an unexpected green stain around the edges. She scrubbed them until they were bright pink. More than once, Eliza looked to the ceiling, not for God, but for her shadow guardian. An inexplicable thrill buzzed in her at the thought of it. She slipped into a clean work dress and tightened her apron. With her hair pinned into a roughly twisted bun, she reached for her ill-fitting cap. The morning breeze gusted more determinedly through the curtains. Eliza closed her eyes and leaned into it. She drew in the strange familiarity of its pungent scent. Refreshed, she knelt to lace her boots only to find the white flower upon the toe of her boot.

Eliza picked it up gently, setting it against her mirror, wedged ever so carefully into a small crack in the old frame. Caught in its reflection, she studied her hazy image, licked her fingers and smeared away a spot of coal from her neck. Deep brown eyes, ringed with green, stared back. Thin dark brows furrowed over them. Full lips pressed white with concentration. The pulse in her neck bounded just above the turn of her collar as she stared deeper at herself, unmoved by the busy footsteps outside her room, uncaring of her duties. She imagined herself dancing with the shadow around the yew tree, threading white flowers through her hair.

As habit demanded, her nails moved to the scars on her wrists, thumbs ready to dig, yet they halted just above her skin. The scars were there, healing in pinks and reds, underpinned with silvery-white, yet around the freshest ones, the skin was dark and dry. She touched a finger to one, its scab flicked away to reveal another rough patch of skin, thick, like bark. Eliza looked to her other wrist; there was a similar change. Her attention swung immediately back to her reflection. The corners of her mouth were tinged a darker hue; they too felt thick and rough. She leaned in closer, looked deep into her eyes. Her irises cracked with a web of black tributaries, encircled in a dark halo. Her pupils dilated, the hairs on her arms stood erect. The voice was no longer in her head; it was within her entire self.

EIGHT

Collecting firewood for the copper held a new joy that morning. Where Eliza used to kick the logs around in fear of spiders, she searched for them instead. She enticed them to crawl upon her hands before leaving them to scurry away in the nearby vegetable garden. Everything felt different, smelled different, as though colour had been punched more vibrantly into the world.

She hummed to herself as she rounded the path back towards the laundry. The sky was bluer than usual, the air headier with nature's odours. Birdsong weaved through the air. She could hear each individual tune where before it was just indiscriminate chirping.

Already unlocked by Mrs Embrey, Eliza kicked the door open and dumped the kindling into a crate next to the copper. It was already warming, but she poked a few extra shards of birch underneath. She added some starch and determined the water needed topping up, so she set about looking for the bucket. It was not behind the door where she usually left it. There were two sections to the laundry room, the clean and the dirty. She fossicked about under the folding and ironing benches first before stepping around the divide to the dirty section —

Eliza grabbed her chest, her knees gave way, vision blurred. She collapsed forward, elbows digging into her thighs, her fingers clawed at her head. Bile rose to her throat, and she vomited up her breakfast. What had been a rare, peaceful start to the day, was now an acidic puddle in front of her. She coughed through the last of the burn, eyes glued to the hook above the wicker baskets full of the sisters' dirty laundry. A howl swirled in her chest; it built and grew. Her cheeks burned; her head thrummed. She drew in the starch tainted air and screamed.

Her cry echoed around the laundry. Eliza raked her chest, trying to claw out the pain.

Eliza heard nothing but her own screams until she felt Mrs Embrey's arms around her. "What? What is it? Have you burnt yourself, child?" The old woman ran her hands hurriedly up Eliza's arms looking for injury. She grabbed Eliza's chin; Mrs Embrey's face was blurred behind her tears of rage. Eliza smelled sugar and vanilla as the old lady's flour-caked hands dabbed her wet cheeks. "Tell me, what has happened, sweet girl?"

Eliza's chin quivered uncontrollably; she grasped Mrs Embrey's wrists. She held tight as something pulled at her, yanked within her as though to take her away. Eliza sucked in a choked sob. Her eyes glanced fleetingly over the old woman's shoulder, and the feeling within took over. Eliza's sobs stopped in an instant, and she stared at the back wall in deathly silence.

Mrs Embrey swivelled her head around. "Oh…oh…oh dearest Lord!" Her voice was thin as she crossed her body, kissed her crucifix, and she pushed herself up. She was unsteady, nearly tripping over her hem as she staggered for the closest bed sheet and draped it over the body of Agnes. The cat hung from a pink ribbon upon a laundry hook, its hair singed away, eyes bulged in the terror of death. Mrs Embrey fumbled to quickly remove the body, mumbling and sniffing rushed words under her breath. As she wrapped up the cat in one of the sisters' dresses, she turned back to Eliza to find her standing, arms stiff by her sides, eyes dilated and fixed upon the swaddled bundle she held in her arms.

"Eliza, dear…" She coughed; her voice choked. "Come, my love, let's put dear Agnes to rest by the rose bushes." Mrs Embrey's voice hitched. "I…I will speak to Mr Blythe about this; he is sure to know how to address this with the Lord. This shall not go unpunished."

Eliza's fingers curled into fists. Her cap slid from her hair that flickered around her face. "Eliza, dear, come now, let's…." Mrs Embrey hesitated as the copper began bubbling wildly. "What the devil?" She hobbled past Eliza, grabbing a round wooden lid. Eliza heard it thud over the boiling liquid, she smelled the fire beneath the copper burn harder.

"Eliza, get up, something's… amiss." Mrs Embrey's voice wavered as she tugged Eliza to leave the laundry. "Come, my love…." Mrs Embrey was cut off as the laundry window exploded. She ducked, but shards of glass left pinpoints of blood across Mrs Embrey's cheeks. Eliza moved not a muscle, just stared ahead, eyes fixated on the hook that Agnes had hung from. Mrs Embrey frantically pulled at her, but Eliza was planted like a tree, rooted in misery.

The laundry smells, so long a balm, were now an assault to her senses. Eliza's face twitched. Her skin itched. Her fingers moved, reached for her arms and scratched, faster and faster until blood wept through the cotton.

"Eliza!" Mrs Embrey cried, still cradling the cat's body against her chest. Eliza grabbed her head, so cluttered with thoughts and sounds, voices, screams, and the image of what poor Agnes had suffered. She could not hear Mrs Embrey's pleas. She ignored Mrs Embrey's hand that pulled desperately at her. Her vision blurred to almost blackness, then cleared, and she stared at Mrs Embrey, tilted her head as though she suddenly did not know who she was.

Mrs Embrey let go of Eliza, grabbed her chest and fell backwards, scrambled back to her feet and crossed herself over and over, but her knees buckled again. "Jesus, Mary and Joseph, Eliza…your, your eyes!"

Liquid filled Eliza's vision; it dripped hot down her cheeks. She wiped a bloody hand across her face. Her skin tarred with inky tears. Her brow creased, confused by the sight, but it did not hurt; it felt... good. She looked back up to the strange woman before her who, for some reason, fell to her knees.

"Dear Lord, preserve us from this evil, please Lord, she may be of no consequence to you and your plan, but she is everything to me," The woman cried.

Eliza felt a twinge in her chest, a warmth. She opened her mouth to soothe the woman, but no sound emerged. Liquid bubbled out instead and drizzled down her chin. The walls creaked, the copper churned its water wildly, the boiling liquid dribbled over the edges as its lid rattled louder.

Mrs Embrey screamed, scrambled to her feet and hit the wall as she backed away from Eliza. "Eliza, pray to the Lord, do it now, child!" She begged.

A fire took hold within Eliza. It burned the strings of servitude and fanned the addictive taste of revenge that flooded the part of her soul left vacant by fear.

Eliza's cracked lips opened again; thick flakes of skin peeled away. A groan rumbled deep inside her chest; a morose scream sailed upon a black vapour that purged from within her. It rose into the air, curled around her. Eliza's fingers clawed at her face; grey skin flecked away in thick woody shards. She reached out towards the woman who cowered in front of her, her palms turned up, each beheld a white blossom in a pool of blood.

Mrs Embrey tripped over a broom before pulling herself up. She ran screaming for help. Eliza's feet moved, drawn along by the private song of her shadow. Her boots moved silently across the path, sank into the softness of the lawn. The shadow encircled her like a vortex, tapped the pain from her soul, drank the last of her fear. As she approached the hedgerow, its branches peeled back in an invitation, the gate ajar.

Eliza stepped through, the hedgerow's branches creaked as they snaked back across the entrance, sealing her off from the here and the there.

NINE

Footsteps rushed through the corridors of Norlane Hall. Servants dashed in and out of every room. Doors creaked open and slammed shut. Desperate shouting in the gardens disturbed the usual calm civility. "Anything?" Someone called. "Not yet!" Another answered.

Mrs Embrey sat by Eliza's window; eyes cast out towards the hedgerow. A gentle breeze fanned the lace curtains about her face. The gardeners hacked at the hedgerow, looking for the strangely absent gate. Footmen, valets, stable keeps and the like all joined together and searched the expanse of the estate for the three sisters.

No one called for Eliza, no one even noticed she was gone. But Mrs Embrey did. Her eyes stung from sleepless nights besieged by nightmares and prayer. Food had lost its taste; she could barely sip tea. With the horror of what she had witnessed in the washroom, Mrs Embrey found no tonic to stop the shake of her hands. She kept them busy, knotting the ribbons she had confiscated from Annabelle's room. Her head tilted left towards the rose garden where she had buried Agnes. Fresh tears dotted the ribbons, not for the sisters, not a single drop. The weight of the house had lifted as though it could breathe without the sisters within it, but Mrs Embrey could not breathe without Eliza. Her tears were for the girl she had saved and lost.

The sound of hooves brought the haze of her aged vision back into focus. Four carts of local villagers, all to look for the sisters, the spoiled brats who had brought nothing but wickedness into the home. Lord Norlane, one arm in a sling, a large rambling stick in the other, greeted the men. Even from the window, she grimaced at the wobble of his jowls and his overindulged paunch. She could almost smell the stale brandy. The search party gathered by the

Grecian statue. Lord Norlane pointed them towards the hedgerow that was imminently about to reveal its secrets as a part of it was cleaved open.

The babe had been grizzling all morning, and now it screamed so loud it penetrated the ceiling. Mrs Embrey glanced up as she rose to her feet, leaning against the wall. Lady Norlane had taken to her bed, unable to pull herself from her melancholy to care for him, not even with the aged Nanny out searching for the wretched girls.

Mrs Embrey wiped her hands down her apron, pulled her cape about her shoulders, ignoring the babe's increasing distress, her mindset on her dear Eliza. As she wandered away from the window, she set about pulling Eliza's bed into order as though this would bring forth good fortune and ease the sick feeling from her belly. As Mrs Embrey lifted, tucked and smoothed the floral coverlet, she noticed something smoking in the fire grate. She reached in with the poker. "Mary, mother of God, please, save my Eliza?" In her hand, she held the remnants of the crucifix.

"The Galdrewold? Surely, they wouldn't have wandered in there again, my Lord? Not after their last misstep?" Mr Blythe questioned Lord Norlane.

"The Devil's work is afoot, man! Do you not see?" Lord Norlane pointed sharply towards the hedgerow. The gate had been located. It was ajar but impassable through the thick knitting of the hedge; the gardeners set to it with axes. The ancient gate was hacked down along with the hedgerow's thorny curtain. Mrs Embrey shielded her eyes as the sun descended, one hand to her fluttering heart. Surely, none of them, even those ridiculous sisters, would have tested the evils of that forest again? She stood within earshot and listened for any snippet about Eliza, but no one mentioned her.

"Boy!" Lord Norlane shouted to the undergardener as the senior one pulled the last of the gate away from its supports.

"How did this happen? Why is the hedgerow overgrown?" His face was plum red, his bulbous nose seemed to grow along with his anger.

"I dunt know what 'yer mean sir," The young boy removed his hat, held it nervously in his hands. He hung his head and wiped the sweat from his brow along a filthy sleeve. "It weren't like this when I tended it this Monday past."

"Hell and the devil! Get out of my sight!" Lord Norlane swung his stick at the lad. "And what of you?" Lord Norlane spun around to the butler. "That blasted gate was unlocked again, Mr Blythe. You have the keys, do you not? Did you not ensure that it was locked and bolted after the other day? Explain yourself man!" Spittle flew from his mouth, and the accusation left the head butler blustering for words.

Mr Blythe's cheeks flushed. "Sir, I have it here," he held up a fat finger, dangling the key upon it. "It hasn't left my person since the other er… incident, My Lord," he cleared his throat and tucked the key back inside his jacket.

Lord Norlane stamped his foot. "Be damned with this." He yelled. "We search the Galdrewold now! Weapons at the ready." Lord Norlane pulled a pistol from inside his jacket and waved it about. Mr Blythe dodged its point.

"A robust reward for whoever finds my daughters safe and well." That and that alone prompted the villagers to verge, and Mrs Embrey was not surprised. A table laden with food, rent that was paid, well, they'd search for Jesus himself. Yet still, no thought of poor Eliza.

She followed the crowd at a hesitant pace towards the hacked hedgerow. All the while, she kept her old eyes sharp for any sign of Eliza; a cap, a shoe, the crucifix from around her neck.

A breeze whistled beyond the hedgerow as the sun lowered in the afternoon sky. Mrs Embrey clutched a small lantern, turning its flame up, as the sky dulled under green-tinged clouds, the air ripe with the smell of more unseasonal rain.

Mrs Embrey watched the glow of the search party's torches dim quickly in the thick of the Galdrewold. She hesitated under the torn branches of the hedgerow, teetered upon the perimeter of the normality of the world she knew and one she feared to tread. In her fifty-six years, she'd not so much as walked along the path towards it. She could not name a single person she knew to have opened its gate without good purpose. It was no place to picnic, not even to hunt.

Her right eye twitched as she noticed a single white bloom with a blood-red centre nestled near the remnants of the doorway; her palms began to sweat.

She had never seen the hedge in blossom. The sight unsettled her further, and she whispered a quiet prayer under the sign of the cross. She reached for the bloom, but a gust pushed her through the entrance, nearly dousing her lamp. Thunder rumbled in the distance. She peered towards the glow of the search party. The air darkened within paces. The smell of roses turned to decay, birdsong dulled to the scratching and slithers of unseen things. Mrs Embrey shivered and hugged herself. The rustling of hidden creatures in a sodden and colourless undergrowth made an old woman's aches a memory and her pace brisk.

TEN

The hoarse voices of the villagers shouted for Margaret, Sybilla and Annabelle in earnest. Nobility and commoner came together for the sisters — still no one called for Eliza.

Mrs Embrey followed the crunch of their footsteps, but their shouts faded away into the vast arena of Mother Nature. Finally, with some distance between herself and the search party, she felt safe enough to call out. "Eliza? Eliza?" No response, no cry for help followed.

Deep shadows ate away residual light as the search party pulled further away. Mrs Embrey rushed, ignored the breathless pressure in her chest. Her eyes squinted in the murky darkness; she only just kept sight of the glow of their torch fire. "Eliza, I'm here. Come out, child, please?" She called less confidently as thunder rumbled closer, sparse fat raindrops began to fall.

"Spread out!" someone yelled in the distance. Mrs Embrey veered right towards the sound. The ambient light of their torches fanned out amongst the thick, ancient treescape; sunset obliterated by its gloom.

"Eliza?" Mrs Embrey's voice hollowed to a nervous squeak. "Eliza, dear, where are you?" She was scared to be heard yet also terrified of remaining silent. She was the voice of the voiceless, and she trudged onward, determined to find her young charge.

The ground became muddier as the rain fell harder. Mrs Embrey pulled her cloak up to shield her head. Water poured down her nose, mixing with the salt of quiet tears. The shouts of the search party tapered away as her old legs tired. She slipped on something, fell to the ground, her lantern doused in the puddle she now found herself in. She gasped, held her hands over her mouth and began to cry out loud. "Please, gracious Lord, bring my girl back to me?" Upon her plea, a guttural scream cut through the wind and rain. That scream was followed by another scream, then a third. Soaked through, shivering, Mrs Embrey tried to pull herself from the mud, but her clothes were heavy, her boots thickly caked. Her heart hammered as more screams ensued. She rolled over, murky puddles splashed into her mouth, the wind whistled in her ears.

Fingers clawed into the ground, she heaved up onto her knees, her body trembled, her remaining teeth chattered. She shook her head with the frustration of age. She was exhausted and fell back onto her side. Lightning lit through the crevices of the canopy overhead; thunder crashed moments later. In the pauses of the storm's wrath, Mrs Embrey could only lay there listening to the distressed cries of whatever the search party had found. "Please don't be you, Eliza?" She mumbled. The wind whipped harder, its whistle more a song in her ear. She could have sworn upon the bible itself she heard a voice in it.

Someone rushed past, followed by another. No one noticed the old lady stuck in the mud and shadows.

"Call for the doctor, man! Hurry, damn you!" Lord Norlane yelled somewhere in the distance. The squelch of their paces died away. They paid no heed to a servant in need of help. One, two, three ran past her, kicking up more mud into her face. She was as invisible as Eliza.

Mrs Embrey prayed for strength as dread iced through her veins. Once more on her knees, a gust swept under her belly and lifted her to her feet every bit as much as if it had hands to do so. She wobbled, grasped a sapling tree to her right, and pulled a boot from the grip of the mud. In the corner of her eye, a shadow dashed by. She gasped, wobbling against the small tree, her hands slipped on the smoothness of its bark, and she slid back down into a fog that rolled in like a tide. It lapped at her feet.

Exhausted, Mrs Embrey leaned back against the tree. She closed her weary eyes and listened to the silence of the Galdrewold that seemed to swallow the shouts of the search party. She would sit there and freeze to death; she accepted this, for her body was now well stuck in both mud and the trappings of her years. A branch cracked, she yelped, eyes wide in the gloom. "Who's there?"

The formless shadow swirled up in front of her out of the fog. It sailed upon the mist; a figure darker than the night. A curl of black smoke reached for her. She screamed; pain burned across her chest and down her left arm. She felt colder. Her vision faded like she was falling into an abyss. The shadow peeled away and hovered. The mist enveloped her, its crisp earthiness melted in each of her breaths and cooled the pain in her heart. Mrs Embrey's eyes cleared, and she regarded the shadow. Malevolence was heavy in the air, it plucked at her skin, tugged at her hairs, yet this thing hovered benignly in front of her as though waiting.

"Are... are you a ghost?" Her voice wavered. The shadow billowed like fanned smoke, but still, it stayed where it was, unaffected by the storm's breath, unpenetrated by the rain. Mrs Embrey tried not to look at it but was drawn to do so despite herself.

She crossed herself again, held her crucifix to her lips. "Do... do you know where my Eliza is?" She felt foolish, reckless even, toying with the forces of the forest. Yet, no one else was here; no one else noticed her. So, she relented to the one thing that had stopped by her side in the mud and cold. "Please, help me?" She whispered. The shadow expanded, stretched tall and thin, its tendrils elongated to resemble arms and legs. It reached out to her but did not make contact.

Mrs Embrey crossed herself twice more. "Lord forgive me, but if the Devil himself helps me find my Eliza, I'll take his hand." She reached out, and the shadow's vapour enveloped her. It lifted her heavy torso, carried her forwards. As terrified as she was by this beast of the Galdrewold, she let it ease her weary bones, guide her old legs, support her thickened waist. The sounds of the storm evaporated, replaced by a song unknown but comforting. It lulled her fear away until the piercing sounds of sobbing cut though the icy wind and pulled the old woman back to reality.

Mrs Embrey breached the thickness of the forest into a murky clearing that the search party's torches struggled to penetrate. She squinted at the blur of people who mingled across on the far side of a raging stream upon an island under the expanse of an immense yew tree. So dense were its branches that it appeared a smudge against the firelight.

"'Tis the Devil's work!" The vicar's gravelly voice bellowed as the wind's whistle calmed its pitch. He chanted the Lord's prayer. Mrs Embrey clutched her racing heart as the shadow pushed her towards a small wooden bridge. Her belly threatened to empty as the odour of rotting meat hit her quite suddenly. Her feet moved one unwilling step at a time. Her first step creaked the boards of the bridge. The whole thing wobbled, but the shadow kept her steady as it lurched. Something creaked rhythmically. She pulled her cape up to her face, smothering the deepening smell of rot. She cleared the bridge. The shadow set her down; her boots sank into sludge on the other side of the raging water, just behind the silhouette of the search party. The shadow unwound from her; fear immediately slithered back through her veins. She followed the shadow's path as it coiled upwards, defying the push of the wind. It wound around the trunk, slithered up and slunk into the recesses of the yew.

That's when she saw the cause of the creaking. A body swung pendulously from a branch. It was small, the dress familiar. Lord Norlane brushed past Mrs Embrey, shears in his hand, another person with a ladder. He froze underneath the rhythmic movement of the body. His shoulders twitched in fits of distress. "My beautiful baby," He collapsed to his knees, the shears fell from his hand. Mr Blythe reached for his employer, but the Lord shoved him away. "Get her down, get her down!" Lord Norlane screamed.

On the lowest branch of the yew, swinging from a plaiting of ribbons, was Annabelle. Mrs Embrey's feet moved without thought until she found herself under the muddied dress flapping against the rigour of Annabelle's legs. A ladder slapped against the branch, and a villager scrambled up it, shears in hand. Others gathered below to catch the body. Mrs Embrey shielded her eyes a moment, but as she heard the metallic scrape of the shears snip open and closed, she pulled her cape away from her face.

The shadow poked about Annabelle's face. It slid into one ear then out the other. It probed at her tongue; a fat slug swollen out from her gaping mouth. Her eyes were bulged and dull. Dried blood crested around dark lips. Mrs Embrey's skin no longer felt the cold; she was numb to the driving rain. The shadow swirled faster as though to show off the sight. No one seemed to notice the apparition or the other murky movements within the tree's knotted top as Annabelle's body thumped to the ground. Lord Norlane threw his coat over the body and hunched over it.

The shadow swirled around the remnant of ribbon before slithering to the ground. Its opaque tip danced away from the tree, bouncing like a tornado looking for the right place to land. It flattened and thinned and writhed silently along the ground towards a curvy stone dressed in moss. Mrs Embrey left her master behind and followed its path. It curled smoothly along the ground as though with purpose. She halted when there was another mortifying cry. "Over here!" Mrs Embrey turned back; her feet ankle-deep in ashy mud. The search party converged on the far side of the yew.

"Help, for the love of God!" A woman hitched her skirt, stepped into the rushing water through waist-high reeds. "Hurry!" Men waded in quickly. They all heaved at a fallen yew branch.

"Can't get her out; she's stuck!" The local Blacksmith yelled over the howling wind. The rain was torrential, the river ran faster, hampering whatever they were doing. "I need an axe," he called, and within moments one was slapped into his hand. Mrs Embrey pushed through the crowd; the shadow coiled between her ankles, through all the muddied feet and slithered beneath the roiling water. Her face drained. She flinched with each strike of the axe against the branch that pinned Margaret's head under the water. Her hair billowed like seaweed, caught in the river's rage.

Lord Norlane stumbled through the crowd; he fell to his knees once more. His ruddy complexion smeared with mud and blood. Snot dribbled from his nose as he reached for his firstborn. "My baby, my beautiful angel," he sobbed, the vicar appeared by his side, holding up his crucifix, chanting continuously.

The branch finally snapped, and her bloated body was pulled ashore. Mrs Embrey backed away. The shadow plumed out of Margaret's mouth, over the crowd, through their flaming torches and back to the mossy rock.

Mrs Embrey followed it as though it held some sorcery over her will. Her mouth was dry, she felt sure to faint at any moment, but the shadow blossomed out towards her, wrapped around her again and gave her a gentle nudge towards the offside of the curvy stone.

She uttered nothing. She felt nothing. She did not reach for Sybilla. She did not remove the stone that crushed her head into the sludge. She watched the shadow circle proudly over its work. Feathers and sticks were matted through the blood-caked remnants of Sybilla's' hair.

All three sisters dead. Hung, drowned and beaten to death.

The shadow swirled upwards and away from the body and sailed away upon the wild wind. Lightning flickered over Sybilla, the contents of her skull a pink mush sinking away into the mud. Thunder cracked close by as her body melded with the undergrowth. She was nothing, just a part of the forest floor for anyone and anything to step upon.

Nausea burned its way up Mrs Embrey's throat. The acidic rumble belched through her tight mouth as she tried in vain to keep the contents within her stomach. She was pushed aside as Sybilla's body was discovered. They jostled Mrs Embrey out of the way; she fell to the ground, vomited and cried.

"Eliza?" she mumbled as she wiped her mouth with her cape. "Eliza?" she screamed. "Where is Eliza? Please, someone, find Eliza?" No one paid heed to her, who would care for a servant, invisible in life and to her terror, in death.

"Burn the tree, burn the whole bloody forest down!" Lord Norlane screamed. Without delay, as the three bodies were carried towards the bridge, the base of the yew tree was set alight. It drank in the heat as though it were tinder on a summer's day, unaffected by the rain and bitter wind. Mrs Embrey's eyes glazed. She watched in silent shock as the flames licked up the trunk and barely heard the vicar's prayers.

The shadow swam through the flames, weaving in and out of the blue and amber heat. It was joined by another, and then another. They swirled together, waltzing through the inferno. The crowd began to dissipate; cold battered Mrs Embrey's back, heat singed the tears from her face.

She felt a hand upon her shoulder. "Come now dear lady, be gone from this place of Satan," The vicar had finally noticed her. She did not budge as he reached down for her hand. Her eyes were fixated upon a new shadow, her arm reached out, her finger pointing to it standing upon the lowest branch that Annabelle had hung from. This shadow seemed calm and unaffected by the flames.

"Eliza?" Mrs Embrey whispered.

ELEVEN

"Fire, fire!" The bell was a distant tinkle that reverberated through the Galdrewold. Mrs Embrey did not move. The vicar left her where she was as everyone raced back towards Norlane Hall.

Under the orange light of the burning yew tree, the shadows of the forest deepened. The rain settled into a soft shower, the wind a gentle breeze, but the tree burned. It crackled and spat; its heat whooshed high into the canopy until a smidge of moonlight found a pathway in. Its light fell upon Mrs Embrey, alone, bewildered. She sobbed silently; her eyes frozen upon Eliza, who stared down, her toes curled over the remnants of the noose rope. Flames ate at her skin, burned the cloth from her body. Her hair billowed until it singed away; she did not move, make a sound of pain, she just stared with piercing red eyes.

"Eliza?" Mrs Embrey whimpered, signing the cross repeatedly over her body. Eliza's mouth opened, and a black mist spewed from within her. It descended upon Mrs Embrey, picked her up and whisked her through the trees, across the mud, through the tingling fog and settled her just outside the remnants of the gate.

The sky was a clear smudge of stars, the air warm and dry. Mrs Embrey coughed on thick, woody smoke. She wobbled on her feet, turned around, hoping to find Eliza behind her, that this was just all a fantastical imagining from shock. But she was alone, the crowd already in a line, passing buckets towards the house. A room in the second storey was aflame.

She moved as quickly as she could towards the house. Her legs burned; her breath barely caught as she hacked on thicker smoke. She stopped to catch her breath at the Grecian statue and looked back over her shoulder. Lightning flashed beyond the hedgerow, fresh rain upon the wind. Thunder rumbled in the Galdrewold as though laughing at the fire it so easily could douse. She grabbed for her crucifix; it felt coarse and strange. She looked down to find twigs and feathers in her palm. An effigy woven intricately hung where Jesus once had. A voice whispered in her ear; she looked up to see the open window of Eliza's room.

Two red slits stared out at her. Mrs Embrey heaved herself up and stumbled closer, each step slow and heavy, each foothold harder than the last. She came as close as she dared. Eliza's head was draped in vines, where hair once was, white flowers dotted through like adornments. Devilish eyes softened towards the old woman; the vines wafted about her cindered skin.

"Eliza? What have you done?" Eliza smiled at Mrs Embrey; charcoal drizzled from her cheeks, and she began to sink away into her room.

"Eliza? Eliza?" Mrs Embrey yelled as Eliza backed away. Mrs Embrey hobbled the last few steps, her hands slapped on the window ledge. As she peered into Eliza's empty room, Lady Norlane's scream pierced from the second storey.

"My baby!"

†

Mrs Embrey rushed through the back door, wet a towel and held it over her mouth. The air burned with every breath. She banged Eliza's door open. The room was empty; a thin layer of smoke floated just below the ceiling. The screams of people tending the flames outside were overwhelmed by another blood-curdling cry from Lady Norlane.

Mrs Embrey coughed and gagged; she spat soot from her mouth as she grasped the balustrade at the first step of the grand staircase. It was hot, and she pulled back. She struggled one step at a time, falling to her knees to crawl upstairs. The smoke thickened into a choking black as she pulled herself onto the landing and collapsed.

Lady Norlane screamed again.

"Give us our child!" Lord Norlane's desperate voice rose above the snapping fire that billowed across the ceiling, the heat melted the joinery of the Venetian chandelier, searing it from its chain. It smashed onto the floral carpet. Mrs Embrey shielded her eyes, but felt the sting of its shards as she inched on hands and knees around the fragments towards the nursery. She vomited, coughed some more and collapsed just inside the nursery door: one eye open, the other blind with soot.

Smoke billowed like thunder clouds; flames licked up the walls. The fire was loud as it whooshed and crackled; its gushes blew more soot into Mrs Embrey's good eye. She blinked with the last of her energy to see the Lord and Lady, both on their knees, huddled near the nursing chair.

"Please, give us our child?" Lady Norlane cried. "You have taken everything else," She collapsed against her husband. That's when Mrs Embrey caught sight of Eliza sitting in the nursing chair, the heir of Norlane Hall contentedly sucking on her charred finger. Her fiery eyes thinned towards her employers. That crescent smile appeared again; flames rose behind the chair in which she sat.

Lord Norlane lunged for his son. Eliza's head snapped towards him, fire arced over the chair and singed away the fingers that had lingered too often where they did not belong. He fell to the ground, curled in a ball and bellowed with agony. Lady Norlane crawled to her husband, not her son.

The fire melted the drapes, seared higher up the papered walls. Eliza gently rocked the child in her charred arms. Her smile widened, splitting her dead flesh, it dripped from her face. Her eyes flickered brighter with delight as she watched the Lord and Lady choke and cower from the encroaching flames. Eliza wrapped the infant tighter in his swaddling as he sucked contentedly. The fire enveloped the base of the chair.

"Eliza… no." Mrs Embrey croaked.

Eliza turned her attention towards Mrs Embrey, the burn of her eyes softened, the wickedness of her smile waned. She opened her mouth and blew towards Mrs Embrey. A white mist, rich with the smell of fresh rain and moss, washed across Mrs Embrey. It cooled her skin, eased the burn of each breath and cleared her eyes. Mrs Embrey pushed herself up onto one hand.

Their eyes held each other for a moment. Mrs Embrey felt every one of Eliza's emotions race through her. She glimpsed every hurt she had endured; felt the weight of Eliza's fury upon the family who had delivered naught but fear and pain upon her.

"Go, child, go," Mrs Embrey laid back down.

Eliza smiled one last time, closed her eyes and rested her head back upon the nursing chair. Haloed in flame, she pulled the babe closer and closer into her chest until it disappeared within her. Flames thickened, their crackle deafening. The walls creaked; the carpet set alight. Eliza smiled calmly before she was consumed by the amber glow.

Fear disturbed the Galdrewold that day. It awoke an ancient wickedness, ignited its appetite and fed it well.

The End

Dear reader,

thank you so much for reading Child of Fear and Fire.

If you enjoyed this story, I would be forever grateful if you could find a few moments to leave a review on Amazon or Goodreads, or other book review platforms. Reviews are always appreciated and help an author's work to be seen. They are the glitter that makes a book shine.

Acknowledgments

Firstly, to my husband and children, who have listened on, yet again, to the constant re-counting of this story as I worked my way through it. Your encouragement and support is forever appreciated. To my beta readers Beverley Lee and Becky Wright, thank you for your patient and considered guidance with developing my story. To Kay Kipling of Full Proof Editing for editing my manuscript to its most polished self. To James and Becky of Platform House Publishing, for my beautiful cover design and interior formatting. Without you all, this story would just be a document on my computer, you all have made it bloom into Child of Fear and Fire.

G.R. Thomas is an Australian based indie author of epic fantasy and dark fantasy. She has had a life-long love affair with books and enjoys creating her own stories out of her dreamscapes and nightmares. G.R. Thomas is a passionate supporter of indie authors. When not writing, she works as a nurse whilst raising her beautiful children along with her husband. An animal lover, she resides on a farm surrounded by a menagerie of all things furry and feathered.

Keep in Touch

Join my newsletter, Spilled Ink, to keep up to date with current works, new releases and giveaways. Sign-up is via my website.

www.grthomasbooks.com

www.instagram.com/grthomas2014

www.tiktok.com/grthomasindieauthor

www.twitter.com/grthomas2014

www.facebook.com/grthomas-author

Printed in Great Britain
by Amazon

79634751R00116